Please return on or before the latest date above.
You can renew online at *www.kent.gov.uk/libs*
or by telephone 08458 247 200

CANNON FOR HIRE

In the autumn of 1897, men flock to the wild Yukon Territory, searching for gold. But Tom Cannon, a one-time cavalry officer, has a different reason for making the hazardous trek north. Hired to find Emmet Lawrence — a greenhorn who'd disappeared seeking his fortune — Cannon searches the icy wastes and snow-capped mountains and draws a blank. No one remembers Lawrence, or knows his whereabouts. Then something happens that Cannon hasn't allowed for — Emmet Lawrence comes looking for him . . .

DOUG THORNE

CANNON FOR HIRE

Complete and Unabridged

LINFORD
Leicester

First published in Great Britain in 2011 by
Robert Hale Limited
London

First Linford Edition
published 2013
by arrangement with
Robert Hale Limited
London

British Library CIP Data

Thorne, Doug.
　Cannon for hire. - - (Linford western library)
　1. Western stories.
　2. Large type books.
　I. Title II. Series
　823.9'2–dc23

　ISBN 978–1–4448–1384–5

Published by
F. A. Thorpe (Publishing)
Anstey, Leicestershire

Set by Words & Graphics Ltd.
Anstey, Leicestershire
Printed and bound in Great Britain by
T. J. International Ltd., Padstow, Cornwall

This book is printed on acid-free paper

1

At first, no one paid much attention to the deadbeat who shoved urgently through the batwing doors of the Paradiso Saloon.

Business was brisk, for this was Friday night and a popular chanteuse by the name of Lula Glaze was due to perform at eight o'clock. The smoke of a hundred cigarettes and half again as many cigars and pipes drifted lazily around the saloon's incandescent arc lamps. The constant buzz of conversation was punctuated by the occasional clink of bottle against glass, the melodic tinkling of the Paradiso's regular pianist as he warmed up on his fine Bechstein piano, and the laddery click of a ball bouncing in and out of the pockets on a spinning roulette wheel.

The newcomer stood just inside the saloon doorway, swaying slightly on the highly polished floorboards. Still no one paid him any attention. After all, such panhandlers were a dime a dozen in this part of town.

But there was something that made this one *different*. This one was bringing news of great importance, and hoping to get a liquid reward for delivering it.

He opened his mouth and spoke a short, single word, but his husky, seldom-used voice refused to carry. The best he could manage was a raw croak. Swallowing, he tried again.

'*Gold!*' he called, and at the word the pianist hit a bum note and stopped playing, and the buzz of conversation dried up, leaving only the roulette wheel to keep turning, the ball still tumbling restlessly from pocket to pocket.

'What was that?' asked one of the patrons, frowning at another. And from the back of the place, 'What did he say?'

'*Gold!*' the deadbeat cried again, enjoying the sudden, unaccustomed attention.

'The *Sacramento Queen* just dropped anchor! She's come straight from Alaska, and she's brought a passel of new millionaires with her!'

At once the conversation started back up, but now there was only one topic.

'You should see 'em!' enthused the panhandler, warming to the subject. 'All them rich men who was poor as church mice but two months ago, just a'comin' down the gangplank tonight like they was royalty!'

The buzz became an animated babble. A few weeks earlier, the *Excelsior* had docked at San Francisco Harbour to disgorge its own batch of fresh-minted millionaires, but most folks were still convinced that the gold rush up in Alaska and neighbouring Yukon Territory was destined to be short-lived, and that the risks of the journey vastly outweighed the potential rewards. Now, though, this second landing seemed to imply that the rush was going to be considerably longer-lasting, and that there was still a good chance to get rich — maybe *very* rich — quick.

Such a prospect galvanized the patrons of the Paradiso. Singly, then by twos, threes, fives and sevens, they began to quit the place, keen now to see the newcomers as they disembarked, and hear their get-rich stories for themselves.

The panhandler hurriedly stepped aside to avoid the exodus. When the saloon had finally emptied out, only he, a slightly bewildered croupier and three dandified bartenders were left: those, and one single customer who was seated at a corner table, smoking a thin black cigar and playing solitaire.

This was Tom Cannon.

Cannon paused to sip some of the aged bourbon in the glass beside him, apparently immune to the gold fever which had so recently swept through the place. The saloon was more like a mortuary now, and somehow he couldn't see Lula Glaze performing with any great enthusiasm for an audience of just one.

That being the case, he abandoned his game, took the cigar from his mouth, drained his glass and reached for his curl-brimmed grey hat, then got to his feet and moved toward the bar with a long, easy stride, fishing money from the pocket of his well-cut grey pants as he did so.

'Barkeep,' he said, nodding toward the panhandler, who was still waiting expectantly to one side of the batwings. 'Give him a bottle.'

With poor grace, for the panhandler had more or less just killed his evening's trade stone-dead, the bartender dispensed the cheer and the panhandler, now looking distinctly shaky, snatched the bottle, hugged it to his narrow chest and nodded his thanks to Cannon.

Cannon himself went out into the misty early evening.

He was a lean but powerful man a notch above six feet, about forty or so, with a square, rugged face and sand-coloured hair cut short to his head. His eyes were grey, his nose short-bridged and straight, his mouth wide, with even teeth. He was dressed in a well-cut brown corduroy jacket, beneath which he wore a freshly-laundered white shirt, a string tie, a tan suede vest.

At this time of the evening, Shell Street was bathed in the sickly yellow glow of the carbon arc lamps that ran the length of the thoroughfare. About fifty yards west, it dropped steeply toward the harbour. At the moment, the mist was still thin enough for Cannon to see the long, sleek lines of the *Sacramento Queen*, with her tall masts fore and aft, and her decks rising one upon another until they reached her two red and black funnels. In the moonlight, the lines of the San Francisco Belt Railway — fifty miles of track that linked every berth down there and made the loading and unloading of ships a slick, speedy operation — glistened like snail-trails.

Closer to hand, Shell Street itself was

in uproar, as word spread and saloon after saloon emptied out and men eagerly made their way down to the harbour. Even a drayman, halfway through delivering barrels to one of the saloons further along the street, had stopped what he was doing to leap back aboard his wagon and whip his horses to speed, almost knocking a little Chinaman to the ground as he went.

Cannon ground the cigar beneath his heel and shook his head. He'd seen all this before, while he was handling an assignment for Senator Sean McCauley up in Seattle. Another steamer had dropped anchor there, to deliver another batch of men who had risked all and come back set for life. Of course, no-one ever spared a thought for the poor sons whose luck hadn't run quite so smoothly, those men who had thought they could fight the land, the elements and a frequently malicious fate to make their fortunes, and discovered to their cost that they could do no such thing.

In any case, Alaska had been yielding

gold now for almost thirty years. Cannon himself remembered Sitka, back in '72, and Juneau eight years later. In the early '90s there had been strikes in the Klondike and at Nome, and just a year earlier, in 1896, a man by the name of George Washington Carmack, his Indian wife Kate, his brother-in-law Skokum Jim Mason and his nephew, Dawson Charlie, had found gold at Bonanza Creek.

When they'd gotten back to Seattle, Charlie had put up at the city's finest hotel and thrown gold out of the windows, drawing a crowd to the street below and causing a fight among the men who felt that those precious nuggets should have been theirs. A few days after Carmack's arrival, another ship had docked, this one bringing home close to seventy men who had also made their fortunes.

Powered by new high-speed presses and telephones, the news had spread far and wide, and the subsequent race to Alaska had shoved even the California gold rush of '48 into the shade.

But suddenly there was no more time for reflection. Cannon sensed movement behind him and turned quickly to face the Chinaman who had almost been knocked down a few minutes earlier.

He was a good-looking man with smooth skin and almond-shaped eyes, about five-six in height, twenty-five or so, and dressed in a fine silk jacket with a penoy floral pattern and frog buttons across the front. Beneath his little blue hat he wore his black hair long, a *queue*, or plait, of it falling from the nape of his neck to trace the line of his spine.

'Mr Cannon?' he asked.

'Who wants to know?'

'I am Kuang-Yi. My mistress would like to meet you. If you would be so kind as to follow me . . . ?'

'Not so fast,' he said. 'Who *is* your mistress?'

'Mrs Lorna Lawrence,' Kuang-Yi replied patiently, as if the answer should have been obvious. 'Her coach awaits us in the alley just yonder, you see?'

With a nod he indicated an alley-mouth about thirty yards away, on the other side of the street.

Still Cannon held back, for the woman's name meant nothing to him. But already he could feel one of his two major failings — curiosity — getting the better of him.

In the end, however, it was the Chinaman who settled the matter for him. 'Please, Mr Cannon,' he said. 'I deliver Mrs Lawrence's request. You come now, so as not to keep her waiting, *shi?*'

And so saying, he turned around and set off along the street, giving Cannon little choice but to follow him.

As he trailed the Oriental, Cannon reached casually into his jacket and eased the single-action Army Colt he carried there in a Hardin shoulder-rig. Built to his own specifications, the gun had a cross-hatched hammer spur for a better grip and a higher, thicker front sight. Each piece had been precisely machined so that the cylinder turned smoothly and the hammer and release worked with unusual speed. As a finishing touch, the weapon had then been sheathed in fine nickel plating.

It was, of course, entirely likely that he was being overcautious. But caution had helped him survive more battles than he cared to remember, from his first savage blooding at the Battle of Powder River right through to the tough and often tumultuous missions he now undertook as a seasoned private soldier-for-hire, and he wasn't about to drop his guard any time soon.

Which was just as well, because even before they reached the darkened alley-mouth, a faint cry cut through the air — the cry of a woman in no small distress.

★ ★ ★

Lorna Lawrence told herself that she'd been a fool to come searching for this man Senator McCauley had recommended to her. Her closest friends had warned her against such foolishness, but she had always been headstrong, and had paid them no heed.

She saw now how wrong she had been.

A tall, attractive, capable woman in her late thirties, she had been content at first simply to await Kuang-Yi's return in the comfort of her rented maroon and black Rockaway carriage. The night was cool, and a faint mist was beginning to drift in off the Pacific.

But then it came to her that this was all taking too long, that Kuang-Yi should have been back by now with the big American in tow.

What *was* the delay? Perhaps this man Cannon was being difficult. Not that she supposed she could really blame him. He wasn't to know what he was letting himself in for by accepting her invitation.

So she decided to wait another five minutes, and then, if there was still no sign of him . . . why, she would go and fetch the man herself!

She sighed heavily. She did not care to be kept waiting, and had never been very good at it. Thus, after only the briefest moment, she gathered her expensive black velvet dress cape around her, and peeling back the netting that fell across her face from the brim of her black and red touring hat, stepped out of the carriage and into the narrow alleyway in which Kuang-Yi had parked the vehicle.

Almost immediately she shivered, for the alleyway was dark and cold, and the mist appeared to be thickening around the Rockaway's twin lamps.

She was about to head for the lights of Shell Street when the horses, which had hitherto been content to stand patiently in the traces, began to fidget.

Stopping, she turned and saw why.

Two men silhouetted against the dismal light at the far end of the alley had just emerged from a shadowed doorway twelve yards away, and were heading in her direction. One was tall, and wore a cap. The other was shorter and fatter, and sported a battered derby. That was as much as she could see in the poor light — but it was enough to send a shiver down her spine.

'Well, lookee here,' said the taller of the pair as they came closer. 'Is my eyes deceivin' me, or does it appear that an angel jus' fell right out of heaven?'

'No, Jake, she's an angel, right enough,' replied his companion. He had a low, husky voice and a manner that seemed eager to please.

The pair shuffled closer. Lorna caught a brief flash of yellow teeth, the glitter of a too-bright eye, as they leered at her. The man called Jake was an emaciated wreck with an overlarge nose and rubbery lips. He, like his companion, wore clothes that were stained and patched, a threadbare jacket buttoned against the chill, ill-fitting pants held up with a length of rope. 'What you doin' so far from home, pretty angel?' he asked.

She made no reply.

'Felt lonely, I 'spect,' opined his friend. His face was jowly and unshaven, his nose little more than a flesh-coloured cauliflower segment set between heavy-lidded blue eyes. It was as impossible to put an age to him as it was to Jake. 'Came down here to find some comp'ny.'

'That it?' asked Jake. 'Is Eben right? You lookin' for comp'ny, lady? A little *excitement*, maybe?'

Trying to stay calm, Lorna glanced over her shoulder, again wondering where on earth Kuang-Yi had gone to, and what was keeping him.

'You know something?' asked Eben, his dry, cracked lips forming into a predatory grin that exposed his gappy teeth. 'I don't think she *likes* us.'

All the while the pair kept edging closer. Lorna, standing tight-lipped, watched them advance and considered turning and making a run for it. But her high-buttoned shoes and her long, blue Arden skirt weren't made for that. She might make a few steps, but then she would stumble and fall, and be theirs for the taking.

But what else could she do? The carriage would provide no protection — it would only offer her assailants cover to do with her as they pleased.

'Get away,' she said at last, her voice low, the fear within it almost but not quite disguised. 'I have a gun in my purse, and I'll use it if I have to!'

It was, of course, a bluff, but it did give them pause for thought, albeit for mere seconds. Then Jake lunged forward and tore the purse from her grasp, moving so fast that she didn't even get the chance to cry out.

'No gun in here, lady,' he said after a brief examination of the purse's contents.

'You *lied*,' said Eben, disapprovingly.

He made a grab for her too, but this time she flung herself back, out of reach, coming level with the Rockaway's front wheel and driver's seat as she did so.

And there, sitting in its socket, no more than eighteen inches from her face, she saw it — Kuang-Yi's slim, bull-hide horse-whip.

Jake pushed past Eben, tired of talk and determined to get at her now, and to prove it he yanked a slim-bladed knife from inside his jacket and brandished it threateningly.

Its appearance spurred her into action. With a cry she tore the whip free, flicked it to its full length and yelled, '*Keep back!*'

Jake and Eben didn't even hesitate this time. They both made a grab for her at the same time, and she took another frantic pace back, brought her whip-hand forward.

More by accident than design, the braided, split-ended whip struck Eben across the left side of the neck. The lash broke skin and sent pain flooding through him. He pulled up sharp, left hand streaking to the injury, his palm filling with blood almost immediately. He swore, swayed, then said with a whole new level of vehemence, '*Get the bitch!*'

Furious now, they crowded her, tore

the whip from her grasp and one of them — she thought it was Eben — fetched her an open-handed slap to the face. Then they were so close that she could smell them, feel the warmth of their unclean breath on her skin, the touch of their grimy hands tearing back the cape, roughly exploring her breasts through the material of her white Chatham blouse —

'No . . . no . . . please . . . '

She might as well have saved her breath, for there was no reasoning with them now and there never had been.

She was dragged forward, slammed hard against the carriage, and while Eben held her tight, Jake brought his knife up, intending to slit the blouse down the front.

Then a gunshot, sounding shockingly loud, tore along the alleyway, and hard on its echoes came the clatter of running feet. Eben swore again, pushed away from her, spun and fled, half-slipping on the damp cobbles.

Jake, however, had other ideas.

Hating to be cheated of his prey now, he bellowed something incomprehensible, then turned to face the new arrivals and flung his knife overarm. It spun past Lorna and went on turning.

Sensing more than seeing it come, Cannon thrust his Oriental companion to the right and threw himself to the left. The knife spun harmlessly between them, lost momentum and clattered to the cobbles a few yards away.

Jake, meanwhile, had turned and was now fleeing, moving so fast that it was all he could do to keep his balance and not tip forward onto his hands and knees. Cannon drew up, lined the Colt on him and knew that even in this poor light he could still wing him. The question was — did he want to?

He didn't enjoy violence and never had, so instead he raised the barrel and sent a second warning shot into the sky, and this sent Jake scurrying even faster.

Lorna swayed as the place of her attackers was taken by her rescuers. Kuang-Yi was glaring at the departing deadbeats, his fists opening and closing. He clearly wanted to go after them, but knew his rightful place was here, beside his mistress.

Lorna, meanwhile, was looking at the man he'd fetched with him. He was taller, heavier, sliding a handgun back into a bullet-heavy shoulder rig.

The minute she saw him she knew who he was, knew that Kuang-Yi had found the man she sought after all.

'M-Mr Cannon . . . ?' she managed.

He looked down at her and nodded. Beneath her touring hat she wore her long, dark auburn hair with a centre part and gathered into a bun. Her skin was flawless and golden, her eyes large, well-spaced, almost amber. She had a button nose and big, undeniably sensual lips.

But it all caught up with her then, the strain of her encounter with the two ruffians, the slap, the gunfire, and her eyelids fluttered. Kuang-Yi saw as much and made to catch her before she fell, but Cannon, moving almost as silently as the mist itself, got there ahead of him, and when she fell it was straight into his arms.

As he scooped her up, he said, 'Does she live around here?'

Kuang-Yi shook his head. 'She has taken an apartment at the Palace Hotel.'

Cannon raised one eyebrow. The Palace Hotel. She must have money, then, a lot of it.

'Let's get her back there,' he decided. 'She's had a hell of a shock, and the sooner we get her somewhere warm and safe, the better.'

2

Lorna Lawrence lay back on an opulent chaise and regarded Cannon with a rueful smile. Twenty minutes had passed, during which they'd gotten the woman back into the carriage and Kuang-Yi, leaping into the driver's seat and taking up the reins, had sped them all back to the Palace Hotel.

Their entrance had been dramatic, with the Oriental, anxious and concerned for his mistress' welfare, clearing the way ahead while Cannon carried her across the lobby toward the elevators as if she were weightless. They rode the elevator to the sixth floor, and at last she was home, stretched out on the chaise.

Kuang-Yi raised the gas, illuminating a large suite furnished expensively, with doors leading off to sleeping quarters and bathroom. It was to the bathroom

that the Chinaman now rushed, returning shortly with a small bottle of
smelling salts, the application of which
began Lorna's recovery. A large glass of
brandy completed it.

Now, over refills, she and Cannon
weighed each other up while Kuang-Yi
made himself scarce. 'You're looking a
little better now than you were ten
minutes ago,' he commented.

'I feel better,' she replied. 'But you
must forgive me, Mr Cannon. I'm not
usually given to fainting.'

'Seems to me you had some justifica-
tion,' he said, indicating the bruise that
Eben's slap had left on her otherwise
golden cheek.

'Even so,' she said, 'I'm stronger than
I look. Shall we get down to business?'

'If you're up to it.'

'I'm up to it,' she insisted, and with a
rustle of petticoats she sat up a little
straighter to prove it. 'Firstly, let me tell
you that you come highly recommended. I wouldn't have wasted my
time in seeking you out if you hadn't.'

'Oh?'

'Yes. Senator McCauley speaks very well of you.'

McCauley, Cannon thought. The old Irish campaigner. Since leaving the army and going into business for himself, he'd worked for McCauley more times that he could remember, often putting his life on the line to achieve the things McCauley could never hope to do through Congress alone.

Suddenly he was wary, because if McCauley had recommended him, he knew that whatever this Lorna Lawrence had in mind wasn't likely to be any walk in the park.

'So what's your problem, Mrs Lawrence?' he asked.

Her smile faded. 'I want you to find my husband, Emmet.'

'He's gone missing?'

'He went up into the Yukon Territory about six months ago, intending to find his fortune. At first he wrote regularly. But then, about three months ago, his letters stopped coming. I thought that perhaps he had found gold, and that the mining or panning of it had taken up all his time. But it also occurred to me that, had that been the case, then he would almost certainly have found some way to let me know of his success first. He would never have remained silent for this length of time. He knows how much I worry.'

Cannon frowned. 'Excuse me, Mrs Lawrence, but you don't exactly seem short of money. Why did your husband feel the need to 'find his fortune', as you put it?'

'Simple. I come from an extremely wealthy family. My husband, by contrast, came from poor but proud stock. It never sat well with Emmet to live off my money. He always expressed the desire to pay his own way, and keep me in the style to which I have always been accustomed. He saw the discovery of gold in the Yukon as a means to do just that.'

'So he went hunting for it and now

he's disappeared,' Cannon said thoughtfully.

'Will you find him for me, Mr Cannon? Senator McCauley says that if anyone can, it's you.'

'I can do a lot of things, Mrs Lawrence, but I can't work miracles. How many men do you suppose have gone north in the last six months? It'd be easier to find a needle in a haystack.'

'If I'd thought it was going to be easy, I'd have done it myself.'

'All I'm saying is that I couldn't guarantee results. In fact, to be perfectly honest with you, I think I'd be wasting my time and your money.'

'But that's the point, Mr Cannon. It is *my* money. And I'd be willing to make it worth your while. I was thinking of something in the region of ten thousand dollars.'

Cannon stiffened. Ten thousand dollars! It was an enormous sum. But almost immediately he reminded himself what he'd have to do to collect it — find one man in an unforgiving wilderness that had a nasty reputation for chewing them up and spitting them out by the hundreds.

'Will you take the job?' she asked. 'Or do I have to find someone else?'

'There *is* no one else,' he said.

He held back a moment longer, intrigued by the challenge the job presented. And that was his second weakness: that he'd never been able to pass up a challenge in his life.

He thought about the Yukon Territory, established by the Hudson's Bay Company fifty years earlier and tucked away in the northwest corner of Canada, where the nights lasted for three months at a time and the temperatures in winter regularly dropped to fifty below.

As the crow flies, it lay twelve, thirteen hundred miles north of Frisco, but considerably further than that by the route he'd have to take. There'd be a 1300-mile sea voyage, for a start, and then another 500 mile trek overland. It was not a journey to be taken lightly. And at the end of it, an impossible mission — to find one man in a land that clocked in at more than 180,000 square miles.

It was a challenge, all right — but as much as he hated to admit it, it was the kind he thrived on.

'I know you can use the money,' she said. 'Your daughter — '

He looked up quickly, and not wanting to talk about that said sharply, 'Do you have any reason to believe your husband might have run into trouble?'

'None.'

'There was nothing strange or untoward in his letters?'

'Nothing.'

'Where did the last one come from?'

'Dawson City.'

He snorted. *It would have to be Dawson*, he thought: the largest metropolis north of Frisco, and home to more than 40,000.

By God, was there nothing about this job that was going to be easy?

'Then that's where I'll start looking for him,' he decided.

Relief washed across her features. 'Thank you, Mr Cannon! Thank you so much!'

'Don't get your hopes up, Mrs Lawrence. The only promise I can make is that I'll do whatever I can to find your man for you, or what's become of him. Other than that, I can't make any guarantees.'

'I understand.'

He drained his glass and got to his feet. 'Well, I'd better set to work. I'll need a photograph of your husband, the best and most recent likeness you have. Then I've got to book passage to Alaska.'

She also climbed to her feet and crossed to a bureau, from which she took a long manila envelope. 'Here,' she said, passing it to him. 'It contains the daguerreotype you need, a draft for five thousand dollars to get you started and a ticket to Alaska aboard the *Angel of Caister*, which sets sail at first light the day after tomorrow.'

He eyed her with new interest. 'You

were mighty sure of me, weren't you?'
he asked. 'Not to mention yourself.'

'That's one of the things about having
money, Mr Cannon,' she replied, and
for some reason she sounded very close
to sad as she said it. 'Sooner or later you
realize that there's almost nothing
you can't buy.'

* * *

The old greybeard with the weather-
beaten face spat a stream of tobacco
juice off to one side. 'I hope to Christ
you fellers've thought long an' hard
about this,' he said, raising his voice to
address the crowd that had gathered
around him. ' 'Cause you've got a hell
of a trek before you, lads, a hell of a
trek, an' you'd best be prepared for it!

'First, there's your passage to Dyea.
That's no picnic! Then the long, long
march over the Chilcoot Pass, a journey
that's already claimed a hundred lives
at least! And after that . . . well, that's
when your troubles *really* begin! You

got to navigate the Yukon River before you can fetch up in Dawson City, an' let me tell you, only the strongest survive in *that* particular hell-hole! Those of you who make it will have to be the toughest of the tough, an' no mistake!'

He ran his crinkly blue eyes across them, a short, stocky old-timer with a thick white beard and wind-reddened cheeks, dressed in a heavy fur coat tied at the waist by a frayed length of rope.

'Still fancy your chances?' he asked.

It was a little after dawn two days later, and the harbour was already bustling beneath a sky the colour of dirty snow. The old man had quickly drawn a sizeable audience, men ranging in age from sixteen to sixty, nearly all of them victims of the country's two recent recessions and the spiraling unemployment they'd brought with them.

No one paid much attention to Cannon, who had paused on the fringe of the crowd to hear what the old man had to say. Neither was there any shortage of advice to be had. Eager to fleece these so-called 'stampeders', loud-mouthed vendors were selling hastily-printed get-rich-quick pamphlets to eager buyers, while a score of outfitters had set up shop along the entire dock to offer everything from rubber hip-boots to navy beans, all at extortionate prices.

'An' the weather!' the greybeard continued. 'Snowstorms that can last a week or more without letup, and cold that's so bad it's been known to freeze a man's blood in his veins! But mark my words, lads, for anyone willin' to risk all, there's riches there for the findin' — and the takin'!'

Cannon, dressed for travel in a lined lamb-leather jacket over a pullover calico shirt and tan canvas pants tucked into high-shaft, low-heeled boots, listened with only half an ear. He had just spotted the *Angel of Caister*, which was presently being loaded with supplies and provisions for the long voyage north.

The vessel was an old, flat-hulled

stern-wheeler about two hundred feet long and forty feet wide. Built of seasoned Douglas fir, cedar and pine, it was probably better-suited to river-work than plying the Pacific Ocean, but right now beggars couldn't be choosers.

'It's a damn' outrage,' said a voice behind him. 'Havin' to pay a thousand bucks for passage aboard that damn' relic!'

He turned to find himself being appraised by a big-bellied man who, like himself, had set his baggage down in order to listen to the old man. He had a hard face and cold blue eyes, and the untidy red hair spilling from beneath his slouch hat was the same colour as his tangled beard.

They started boarding a little before seven. Cannon dragged his gear up the gangplank. He'd spent the previous day preparing for the trip. He'd written to his wife, who was presently living in Maryland, then gone out and bought everything he was likely to need for this mission — heavy-knit underwear, socks,

33

overshirts, a sweater, spare blankets, a mackinaw and mittens. He'd also fetched along his Winchester Model 1887 lever-action shotgun, not because he was expecting trouble, but because in wild country like the Yukon, a man could never guarantee he wasn't going to run into it.

A crewman carrying a soot-stained lantern led him and his fellow passengers below decks to a large but Spartan public room that would be their quarters for the next six days. The room was ill-lit, its dull yellow walls and low ceiling darkened still further by an accumulation of nicotine. Narrow cots had been set out in three long ranks so that it could sleep up to eighty men.

Cannon grimaced at the ill-disguised smells of urine and sweat that a recent steam-cleaning hadn't quite been able to shift, but once again reminded himself that few were making this journey in comfort right now. The shipping lines were packing in as many gold-seekers as possible and charging top dollar for the questionable privilege.

Someone shoved an elbow into Cannon's back to keep him moving. Glancing around, he recognized the redhead who'd earlier complained about the condition of the ship. He shrugged. He allowed any man one shove. After that he usually started shoving back.

He selected a corner cot and threw his baggage under the thin mattress. Around him, other men made similar claims of their own. 'Hurry up, there!' yelled the sailor. 'We put to sea in less than thirty minutes!'

True to the prediction, the ship's twin stacks began belching charcoal-grey smoke within the half-hour, and then the ship's whistle let go a shrill blare. Ropes as thick as a man's neck were unknotted and cast off, and then the vast iron wheels attached to the stern began to turn, slowly at first but then with greater purpose as their wooden paddle blades scooped down into the water to provide the necessary thrust to get them moving.

On deck, men cheered and waved to loved ones and cried final farewells that were drowned by a thousand other sounds. Cannon crossed his arms on the guardrail and watched as the San Francisco skyline shrank before them. A strong wind sprang up, rocking the ship with the force of a seven or eight on the Beaufort Scale. The sky was grey, for it was already September and Indian summer had yet to make its last stand before yielding to autumn.

He was just about to go below decks again when he heard voices behind him and glanced around. A few yards away stood the old greybeard who'd been holding forth on the jetty earlier. He was now accompanied by a thin lad of about seventeen or so. Cannon didn't hold out much hope that either of them would survive the hardships that lay ahead.

The old man said something and clapped the boy on the shoulder. The boy tried to smile but couldn't quite manage it. He was pale-paced and hollow-cheeked, dressed in threadbare pants and jacket, his mouse-brown hair cut short and ragged, with an untidy fringe showing beneath a rabbitskin cap.

The wind blowing off the Pacific stirred up white crests and showered the decks with icy spray. Cannon turned his collar up and hurried below.

⋆ ⋆ ⋆

Towards early evening, the clouds darkened still further and they sailed into a storm that tossed the ageing vessel around like so much driftwood.

A short time earlier, the galley-staff had ladled out a thin-looking soup to those brave enough to eat it. Now, as the ship lurched and plunged, more than a few had to stagger topside to throw it back up.

Cannon managed to keep the meal down and tried to sleep through the worst of it, but it was impossible. As seasoned a traveller as he was, he quickly developed a headache, but worse than that, he was suddenly consumed by a restlessness he knew only too well, and against which he was powerless.

He was forty now, and though it was what he did best, he'd had his fill of soldiering. But fate, as he had discovered to his cost, had other ideas.

Having lost his parents in a cholera epidemic when he was sixteen, he'd enlisted because he could think of nothing else to do. Once in uniform, however, he'd discovered a natural aptitude for soldiering that had eventually brought him to the attention of General George Crook himself.

Under Crook he'd seen action at Powder River, the Rosebud and the Little Big Horn. Later, under the command of Nelson A Miles, he'd chased Geronimo from one end of the Sierra Madres to the other. In his time he'd fought Sioux, Cheyenne, Nez Percé, Apache, Kiowa and Comanche, and with General Crook's patronage he'd also achieved the near-impossible — he'd risen steadily through the ranks from private to corporal, from corporal to line sergeant, then first sergeant, then second lieutenant, first lieutenant and finally captain.

But everything had changed when he met Beth Drummond, the raven-haired eldest daughter of Fort Bowie's sutler. Beth was the first really *peaceful* thing that had ever happened to him, and she had made him realize that after twenty years, he'd had his fill of fighting.

The couple had married within the year, and shortly thereafter Cannon mustered out, bought an ailing horse-ranch up in the Chiricahua Mountains and set about supplying the army with remounts. Little over a year later, Beth gave birth to their only child, Amy.

In the darkness of the public room, the planes of Cannon's face suddenly hardened.

Amy was a beautiful child, so small but so quick to learn, her round, red face crowned by hair as midnight black as her mother's, her eyes soon settling to the same gunsmoke-grey as his. As the months progressed she learned to crawl and explore, and communicate after a fashion. She was a constant source of surprise and joy.

But then she fell ill with scarlet fever.

Oh, she got over it, of course. But she seemed strangely vague after that, she cried a lot, and every time Beth picked her up she went stiff and her fingers splayed and she grew scared. Where before she'd been lively and inquisitive, she now lay still, her manner withdrawn and guarded.

Anxious to dispel their growing suspicions, they took her to Fort Bowie so that the army surgeon could examine her, and that was where they had their worst fears confirmed.

'There's no easy way to say it, Tom, so I'll just come right out with it,' said the physician, once he was finished. 'Amy's what we call deafblind.'

Before she could stifle it, Beth

sobbed just once. Cannon glanced at the floor, his whole world tilting unpleasantly.

'The scarlet fever affected her in a way we don't yet fully understand,' the surgeon continued gravely. 'My guess is that it was complicated by something else, something we didn't pick up on at the time, maybe rheumatic fever, maybe secondary scarlatinous disease. Anyway, I'm sorry to say that it's left her with hardly any sight and no appreciable hearing.'

Silence filled the infirmary for a moment, as Cannon looked across at his daughter, trapped in a dark, silent world with no understanding of where all the light and sound had gone. Then Beth asked haltingly, 'Is it permanent?' Her voice caught a little as she said it.

The doctor shrugged. 'That I can't say. Frankly, her condition is beyond the understanding of an army surgeon.'

'But not beyond the understanding of a specialist?' Cannon prodded hopefully.

The surgeon looked out the window at the dusty parade ground beyond. 'Not beyond the understanding of an *expensive* specialist,' he replied.

Cannon waved that off. Money was the least of his concerns just then. First they had to find out the true extent of the damage, and whether or not it could be put right. 'Where do we start?' he asked.

'I'll make some enquiries, send a few wires, write a few letters. If there's anyone out there who can help, I'll find him for you.'

'Thanks, Chuck. I appreciate it.'

The army surgeon was as good as his word. About a week later he sent a dispatch rider out to the ranch with details of the Abbott Institute for the Advancement of the Deafblind, in Baltimore. As soon as they raised enough money to make the trip, they travelled to Maryland and allowed the principal, Dr Benjamin Abbott, to examine Amy for himself.

'I'm afraid that the situation is even

worse than I was led to believe,' said the doctor, a tall, thin man of about sixty, who had longish white-grey hair and round, wire-framed spectacles. 'In addition to being deaf and blind, your child has also lost her sense of smell and taste.'

Beside Cannon, Beth sagged.

'Can you help her?' he asked.

'Oh, certainly. But I cannot *cure* her: at least, not yet. An operation that would somehow give her back those senses she has lost is presently beyond medical science. But that may not always be the case. I am in contact with colleagues all over the world, and we are learning new things, new techniques, every day. The moment there is a breakthrough in the restoration of any one of her lost senses, or some promising new form of treatment, I will know about it — and implement it.'

'Then what can we do in the meantime?'

Abbott looked down at Amy, who was laying quiet and still in her wicker baby carriage. 'The first thing we must do is find a way to communicate with her, and for her to communicate with *us*. Initially we will have to reach her by *touch*, teach her to communicate with finger signs and gestures. But it will not be easy. And I am sorry to say, Mr and Mrs Cannon, that it will not come cheaply.'

'I didn't expect it would,' Cannon replied. 'You just tell me how much it's going to cost to enrol her here and let your people work on her, and somehow I'll pay it.'

Dr Abbott made some calculations, then named a figure for the year. For that, he said, Amy would receive the finest residential care and the best and most up-to-date treatments available. Maybe even more importantly, she would be among her own kind.

Cannon fell silent. Although he tried to hide his surprise, nothing could have prepared him for such an amount. But how could he call himself a father and not at least *try* to raise the money?

For a while after they left the Institute, he felt powerless and hated the feeling, because he'd spent his whole life facing enemies he could fight in ways he could understand. What he didn't know about fighting and winning those fights could be written on the inside of a thimble. But here was an enemy he couldn't fight in any way he knew.

Or *could* he?

They needed money, a lot of it. And out there, 1,500 miles west of genteel Baltimore, on a frontier that was still wild and woolly, a fighting man of his quality could command top dollar.

Of course, after two decades he'd had enough of that kind of life. But what did they say? Needs must when the Devil drives.

Well, the Devil was certainly driving him now. So Cannon made a decision. He'd sell the ranch, set Beth up in a house close to the Institute, then head back west and start selling his gun to the highest bidder, always in the hope he could earn enough to give Amy the chance at life she deserved.

Like it or not, Tom Cannon was going back to war.

3

The following day the weather calmed enough for Cannon to take some air on the *Angel's* main deck. The dawn sky was milky and the rising sun showed like runny egg-yolk through the thin, drifting clouds.

The old greybeard was already on deck, resting against the capstan and gazing thoughtfully off to starboard, where Oregon's rugged coastline could just be seen as a jagged grey-green line on the horizon. The muffled chug and throb of the engines beneath them made the deck vibrate like the ribcage of a dozing dinosaur.

The old man looked around when he realized Cannon was watching him. He was at least seventy, but in the light of a new day Cannon had to revise his earlier assessment of the man. He might be old, but there was something about him that was tougher than whipcord.

'Hell of a storm last night,' he said by way of greeting.

'Been through worse than that,' the old man replied.

'I figured as much.'

'Oh?'

'I was in the crowd yesterday morning, heard what you had to say about things up in the Yukon. You sounded like a man who knows what he's talking about.'

'I should do. I've spent damn'-near half the past ten years there.'

'Mind if I ask why?'

The old man shrugged. 'Man has to do somethin' with his time.'

'At your age, I'd have thought you'd be taking it easy by now.'

'Never had the inclination for that. Guess I was always too busy wonderin' what's on the other side of the mountain.'

'And you're still curious, is that it?'

'It's what keeps me goin'.'

'Ever had any luck up north?'

'Oh, I've had my strikes,' declared the greybeard. 'Trouble is, I find it, I mine it, I turn it into cash and then I spend it. Not much else to do after that but go back an' do it all over again.'

Cannon produced two thin black cigars and offered him one. The old man said, 'Don't mind if I do.'

When they had the smokes lit, he added, 'Henson Moore's the name.'

'Tom Cannon.'

They shook.

'You don't look much like a stampeder to me, Cannon,' Moore opined, eyeing him shrewdly. 'Any man can afford such fine cigars and a right fine jacket like that doesn't need to dig or pan for gold.'

'You'd be surprised.'

'Naw. You don't fool me none. But if gold's not your game, what takes you north?'

Cannon hesitated. Then, deciding to take a chance, he said, 'I'm looking for a man. He's gone missing and his wife wants to know what's become of him.'

The old-timer scratched thoughtfully at his beard. 'He got a name, this man?'

'Emmet Lawrence.'

Moore considered it for a moment, then shook his head. 'Never heard of him. What's he look like?'

'Here,' said Cannon, showing him the daguerreotype.

The old man studied the picture for a while. A studio portrait, it showed an even-featured man in his late thirties, clean-shaven and smartly-dressed, with pale, cool eyes and a sober, unsmiling mouth. He had thick hair, dark and oiled, with a centre-parting.

'Sorry,' said Moore, handing it back. 'But I can ask around, iffen you like. It's a long shot, but mebbe some o' the crew might remember him.'

'I've got nothing to lose. The last time his wife heard from him he was in Dawson City, but that's all I've got to go on.'

'Well, we'll see what we can turn up for you. You ever been to the Yukon before?'

'No. But I've known cold. I suffered frostbite once, up in Montana Territory.'

'Montana, huh?' Moore repeated speculatively. 'Well, you think about what winter was like up in Montana, then multiply that by three or four, an' then you'll get a vague notion of what you got waitin' ahead of you.'

'Sounds ominous.'

'It should. But you strike me as an all-right feller, so I'll tell you what. You stick with me when we get off this tub an' I'll get you safely through to Dawson.'

'Appreciate it.'

'Ferget it,' said Moore. 'There's safety in numbers, Cannon. An' where we're headed, a man without a friend to watch his back'll be lucky to last out the week.'

* * *

The *Angel of Caister* continued to push north over the next several days, always hugging the misty coastline. The rocky capes of Washington eventually gave way to the fjords and valleys carved into the shores of British Columbia, and shortly thereafter the waters of the Pacific yielded to those of the Gulf of Alaska.

On the fifteenth day they reached Dyea.

The town looked poor and unpromising. Set just beyond the churned-up beach, it seemed to be a messy sprawl of hastily-built log shacks, stores, flophouses, restaurants and dancehalls set between narrow, almost impassably-muddy roads. Smoke rose from rock chimneys in thin, wind-whipped lines, and beyond them, tall, snow-etched mountains rose skyward until their peaks were shrouded in mist.

The sternwheeler dropped anchor about forty yards from shore and a bright blue whaleboat was lowered into the dirty grey water alongside it. Since the town had no dock, the passengers and their gear had to be ferried to shore by crewmen who charged two dollars a head for the service.

While the first batch of gold-seekers took their place in the whaleboat, Cannon caught sight of the young lad he'd seen Moore addressing shortly after they left San Francisco. He seemed to be lost in the crowd, not quite sure where he was or what was expected of him.

Moore spotted him too, and tutted. 'Now, there's a *cheechako* if ever I saw one,' he murmured. 'If I don't take him under my wing, he'll be dead for sure by the end of tomorrow! What say we keep him close an' get him through this?'

By way of reply, Cannon indicated with a wave that the youngster should join them. The lad was so over-awed by what was going on around him that he didn't notice at first. Then Cannon caught his eye and he quickly elbowed his way over.

'Yessir?' he asked timidly.

'Stick with us, button,' Moore said

kindly. ' 'Lessen you've had a better offer, we'll see you through.'

The lad's eyelashes flickered with relief. 'I'd 'preciate it,' he said, offering his hand to each of them in turn. 'I'm Tyson, by the way. Jeffrey Tyson.'

Introductions made, the three took their place in line, throwing their bags down to the crew of the whaleboat when their time came, then climbing awkwardly down a rope ladder to join them.

It didn't take long to cross the bight, and soon they were grabbing their gear and wading through the surf up toward what the people of Dyea chose to call their main drag. A few townspeople wrapped up against the icy blasts that came in off the sea had gathered to watch the newcomers trudge ashore. Cannon looked into their faces and saw ill-concealed greed in almost every one. These would be the merchants, saloon-keepers and owners of Dyea's few boarding houses, trying to gauge what this latest batch of newcomers would be worth to them.

'We'll club together with some of these other fellers an' find ourselves a room for the night,' Moore decided. 'We'll never be able to afford one, just the three of us. Then we'll stow our gear and buy supplies for the journey. Best be quick about it, too. There won't be much left for any Johnny-Come-Latelies.'

Because he was an old hand at this kind of thing, Moore managed to agree a not-too-extortionate price for their supplies, and when they headed back to the tiny cabin they and ten other men had rented between them, they were weighed down with navy beans, bacon, flour, rolled oats, corn meal, rice, sugar, tea, coffee, baking powder, baking soda, condensed milk, beef extract, candles, borax and evaporated fruits, onions and potatoes. It seemed to Cannon that they'd bought far more than was practicable, but Moore assured him that the Canadian authorities would only allow them to cross the border if they were packing sufficient food and supplies.

With the coming of dusk the temperature dropped like a rock, and even the small fire they managed to light in the stone fireplace had little effect against the blood-stopping cold. Sleep was close to impossible, even swathed in blankets as they were, so the ever-garrulous Moore decided to put the time to good use by preparing his companions for the events of the coming days.

'I can't speak for the rest o' you men,' he began, 'but we three're takin' the trail over Chilcoot Pass on up to Lake Bennett. White Pass is too damn' troublesome.'

'Maybe it is,' said a big man with broken teeth, whose name was Grady. 'But aboard the *Angel* they told me we could walk it with horses and oxen! I reckon that should get us to Dawson all the sooner — and get us out of having to carry our own gear!'

There were a few murmurs of agreement from Grady's companions, but Moore only shrugged. 'You're right,' he allowed. 'You'll forge ahead with horse and wagon — for the first few days. But then you'll come to a dead stop.'

'Why?' demanded the surly redhead. His name was Sweeney and as soon as he'd come ashore he'd headed straight for one of Dyea's many saloons, there to slake the thirst he'd built up since leaving San Francisco. As a consequence he'd left buying his supplies to the last minute, and now he wasn't packing anywhere near enough.

'Because you'll have reached swampy ground,' declared Moore. 'Then rivers, then mountains. All the way from there you'll be trying not to break your necks in one chasm after another, an' then you won't even manage a walkin' pace! I've taken that trail myself, an' seen it happen. Men, animals . . . it's not a pretty sight.

'Remember this, too,' he went on. 'It don't make a damn what you used to be back in the States. Out here you're all what they call *cheechakos*, what we call greenhorns back home. An' there's plenty of coldblooded, hard-hearted rogues who prey on *cheechakos* right the way along the White Pass.' He showed his yellow teeth in a grimace. 'If the Pass doesn't get you, make no mistake about it. *They* will.'

Moore's pronouncement had a sobering effect on the men around him, and it fell quiet but for the crackle and spit of the fire. Turning his attention to Tyson, who was huddled in brand-new store-bought blankets beside him, he said confidentially, 'Not too late to turn back, iffen you're havin' second thoughts. There's not a sensible man here who'd blame you.'

'Mr Moore,' Tyson replied earnestly, 'I got no choice, not if I want to make a better life for my wife an' me.'

'Even if it means turnin' that wife into a widow?'

'You don't understand. Susan and me, we married against the wishes of her folks and mine. I told 'em I'd look after her, but they never did think I'd amount to much, and I guess they were right.

'Back home I picked oranges for a living. Where's the dignity in that — or the money? If Susan hadn't taken a job in the local jute mill we'd have starved for sure, an' unless I make some money soon, it looks like we'll be close to starving again.'

'Why's that?'

'Because she's in the family way,' explained Tyson. 'An' she won't be able to work at all after the baby's born.'

'So you figured to make your fortune up north?'

'I've been reading about it for months now, about how there's gold for the finding in the Yukon Territory. Didn't think I'd ever raise enough money to go there an' find it for myself, of course, but then one of Susan's aunts died an' we came into a little money. Not much, but enough to pay my way north.

'So now you see why I'm not turning back, Mr Moore. It's because I'm set on striking it rich an' making it up to Susan, providing for the baby an' proving her folks an' mine wrong.'

Cannon thought about Emmet Lawrence, a man who'd gone north in the hopes of supporting his own wife: a man who'd then vanished, maybe for good.

'Well said,' replied Moore. 'But if you're determined to see it through, button, let's get a couple things straight right at the outset. First off, you don't call me mister. No one does. I'm Moore, or I'm Henson. Got it? Second, you been warned. When it gets rough out there, I don't want no complainin'. If you break down on the Chilcoot Pass, you die where you fall, you hear me? And thirdly . . . '

'Sir?' Tyson asked nervously.

Moore grinned at him. 'Never say die, boy, and you'll do just fine.'

         *   *   *

For the next five days they marched from dawn till dusk. The trail always seemed to wind uphill, and though most of the men grumbled, Henson Moore made no comment, just saved his breath for the climb. Cannon began to get a new appreciation of the man, for despite his advancing years he really was as durable as fine leather.

'Hey, Moore!' called Sweeney, who had elected to come with them. 'Just how far is this mountain peak? I'm about all in!'

The old man glanced over his shoulder. 'We won't see her for a while yet!' was his reply.

They made camp late in the afternoon, choosing a stand of skeletal trees whose bare branches were loaded with settled snow. Campfires were made, coffee boiled, beans heated through, bottles of brandy passed around to help combat the bone-deep chill.

'You never did answer Sweeney's question,' called one of the would-be gold-diggers, whose name was Purdue. 'Just how far till we reach this peak you was tellin' us about?'

Moore sampled a spoonful of beans from the pot suspended over the fire he was sharing with Cannon and Tyson. 'Maybe another five days.'

Some of the listening men groaned, swore or did both. Ignoring them, Moore went on, 'I'll tell ye somethin' else, besides. The last four miles'll be the worst!'

'Are you kiddin'?' demanded Sweeney.

'It's four miles uphill all the way,' Moore pointed out. 'And you're carryin' all you possess on your backs, in bad weather!' He grinned. 'Everywhere you look you'll find ice. One wrong or careless step an' you're done for!' He shook his head. 'Yup — just four lousy miles . . . but I'm thinkin' it'll separate the seed from the chaff in this bunch!'

4

Five days on they reached Chilcoot Pass. It lifted before them across a great, broad sweep of a rise with pristine snow covering it like a pure white tablecloth.

According to Moore, however, appearances were deceptive. For beneath the smooth snow lay a miles-long jumble of sharp-edged, slate-grey rocks and loose shale, the result of some eons-old avalanche, and at its peak it squeezed tight to fit between mountains shaped like buffalo humps fashioned from great, rough chunks of ice. Those mountains were the barrier that separated American soil from Canadian.

The gold-seekers gathered at the foot of the pass and studied it the way they might study an opponent. 'I'll be damned,' breathed Purdue, craning his neck. 'You ever seen the like before?'

No one had.

Studying the misty summit, Sweeney called, 'Where are the Mounties, then, Greybeard?'

'They're up there, don't you worry,' Moore assured him. 'An' like I've been tellin' you ever since we hit Dyea, they'll turn back any man here who doesn't have enough provisions.'

'Well, I don't see 'em up there,' insisted Sweeney, thumbing at his red beard.

'Then make the climb,' invited Moore, fixing him with a hard look. 'But don't come cryin' to me when they turn you around and send you back where you came from.'

Sweeney stiffened. 'I know how much I need to get by on,' he growled. 'An' I'll not be dictated to by any damn' redcoat.'

Moore, who knew better than to argue with him, just shrugged and turned away.

Since the afternoon was already well advanced, and thus too late to begin the tortuous climb, they lit fires, raised tents and boiled up coffee and beans, and most decided to get an early night in order to be as fresh as possible for the morrow.

Sweeney, however, was the exception. Enjoying one last smoke before climbing into their blankets, Moore elbowed Cannon and indicated the redhead with a nod. 'He's havin' second thoughts at last,' he whispered. 'Goin' around tryin' to buy extra supplies from the others.'

It was true. Sweeney was stopping at man after man, group after group, and offering money for a sack of beans here, a side of bacon there. Judging from the reception he was getting, however, few men were in any mood to sell, and eventually Sweeney, empty-handed and cursing, stamped angrily off into the night.

Just before dawn the next day the party broke camp and once again gathered at the foot of Chilcoot Pass. Ever since Dyea, they had come to look upon Moore as their unofficial leader, and it was Moore who now gave the order to move out nice and slow.

It was sound advice, for as they began their ascent, the men realized that sandwiched between the snow and the rocks lay a more or less solid sheet of ice. They had to lean forward and dig in every step of the way, and every step of the way hope not to fall flat on their faces.

What made things worse was the fact that the higher they climbed, the steeper the trail became. Men sweated and swore. More than a few had to fall out, flop to the ground and catch their breath in great, steaming heaves. Progress was slowed still further when two men were injured in minor but awkward falls, one breaking his right arm, the other twisting his right ankle.

Somehow morning tipped over into afternoon. When they were about halfway up the incline, the mist lifted slightly and Cannon spotted a stout log cabin at the summit, set to one side of the trail, its roof cloaked with snow, the smoke from a fire rising from its stone chimney to be shredded by a sudden, icy blast of moaning wind. He couldn't see anyone around up there, but it was a safe bet that the Mounties had seen them coming from the cabin's small windows.

As early dusk finally began to settle and more bad weather began to close in, lamplight filled those same windows and someone up there lit a bonfire as a sort of beacon for the climbers. By its light Cannon saw four men wrapped in heavy coats watching as they tackled the last stage of their ascent.

Moore was the first to reach the rugged frontier station, followed closely by Cannon and then a hard-gasping Jeff Tyson. Sweeney, meanwhile, deliberately hung back and tried to lose himself in the growing darkness.

Three of the Mounties were young, inexperienced-looking constables. Cannon figured this was probably their first posting. The fourth was older and tougher, with a round, wind-burnt face and a small, dark moustache. He introduced himself as Sergeant Angus MacLeod.

In threes the stampeders were taken into the cabin, asked their names, where they were from and whether or not they had any infirmities or other ailments. Finally, the constables checked their provisions to satisfy themselves that each man was carrying enough to survive. Then Cannon and his two companions were allowed back out into the wind-whipped darkness and wished good luck.

No sooner had they left the cabin than a figure appeared out of the shadows beyond the bonfire to join them. 'Come on, fellers,' hissed Sweeney. 'Let's get out of here.'

Before they could respond, a stern voice bawled, 'Not so fast there, laddie!'

Sweeney turned as MacLeod stalked over and fixed him with a glare. 'You're not going anywhere!' he said. 'Look at your pack, man! Don't ye know ye've too few victuals to be allowed through?'

Another man might have tried diplomacy, but Sweeney was not another man. He was bull-headed and stubborn as a mule, and his unpredictable, hair-trigger temper was by now well-known to his companions. 'Don't you worry yourself about old Sweeney,' he replied. 'I'll make out. I've done fine up till now.'

'I hate to dent such fine confidence,' said MacLeod, 'but we have rules out here, and it's my job to uphold 'em. Now, you're welcome to shelter in yonder barn for tonight, but unless you can conjure up some extra supplies by morning, you'll be starting back to where you came from. Got it?'

Sweeney planted himself and stuck out his jaw. 'I hope you're just sayin' that, bud, an' don't intend to enforce it! I didn't come all this way just to be turned back!'

MacLeod brought up the billy club he'd been holding. 'You'll be turning back,' he said deliberately. 'The only question is whether or not you'll be carrying a few extra lumps with you when you go.'

Sweeney's eyes hooded. 'Best not to try puttin' the frighteners on old

Sweeney,' he said in a low, dangerous voice. 'Else — '

MacLeod didn't give him the chance to say any more. He brought the billy up and struck Sweeney a blow alongside the head, and though Sweeney's fur hat cushioned the worst of it, he went down fast nonetheless.

With a sorry shake of the head, MacLeod bent, grabbed him by his collar and started to haul him away, but once again Sweeney showed that he had other ideas. Groggy but still conscious, he reached into his pocket and brought out a blued, short-barrelled .45, and before anyone could do or say anything to stop him, he stabbed it at the Scotsman and shot him point-blank in the chest.

MacLeod slapped down hard into the snow with his arms outflung and his billy club flipping through the air to land at Cannon's feet.

Sweeney, meanwhile, staggered up onto his knees and quickly brought the weapon around to cover MacLeod's three constables as they reacted to the shot. 'Not a move!' he barked through clenched teeth.

The silence that followed his words was broken only by the hissing of snow as it landed in the bonfire. By its flicker Sweeney's face appeared flushed and desperate, and there was a little blood around his left ear. 'Stay back, you damn' Canucks!' he screamed. 'Or so help me I'll kill you all!'

For a long, strained moment there was neither sound nor movement. Then one of the constables raised his empty hands and took a pace forward. 'Drop that gun before you make things worse than they already are!' he called.

Sweeney thumbed back the hammer. It made a loud, ratchety sound. 'Not a chance!' he grated.

The constable backed off, though it was clear from his expression that he hated having to do so.

Then Cannon called urgently, 'Sweeney!'

Instinctively Sweeney turned to face him, and as he did so, Cannon threw the billy club he'd picked up while Sweeney was busy with the Mounties. It blurred forward and struck the redhead full in the face, connecting with a dull pop of sound, and Sweeney grunted and then fell over backwards, bleeding from his freshly-broken nose.

In seconds the three constables had him surrounded. They relieved him of his gun and then two of them dragged him away, leaving the third to make a hasty inspection of his fallen sergeant.

'Thanks, mister,' he called over one shoulder.

'Forget it,' said Cannon.

'Anyone here know anything about gunshot wounds?'

The watching gold-seekers shuffled their feet, either unable or unwilling to get involved. Reluctantly Cannon said, 'I've watched army surgeons work on 'em. But I'm more likely to kill him than cure him, if that's what you've got in mind.'

'He'll die for sure if he's left untended,' snapped the constable, and

Cannon realized that what he lacked in experience he more than made up for in determination. 'So you got nothing to lose.'

Cannon shrugged off his gear and said, 'Help me get him inside. Henson, you'd better come too. You got a medical chest, constable?'

'No.'

'*What?* No forceps? Pincers?'

'Not that I know of.'

'All right. I'll need scissors, soap, water, some rags. You've got that, I suppose?'

'Of course.'

'Got any rubbing alcohol?'

'No.'

'Whiskey?'

'Some.'

'That'll do.'

They carried the wounded man into the cabin, where it was warm and light. At Cannon's order, Moore hurriedly cleared the table in the centre of the room and they stretched the patient out on it.

While the constable fetched extra lamps, Cannon pulled off his mittens, took off his jacket and knelt beside the base burner stove, flexing and unflexing his fingers to get them working again.

Finally he returned to the table and carefully unbuttoned the wounded man's coat. MacLeod had been shot in the upper right torso, about three or four inches below the shoulder. His crimson serge tunic was sticky with blood.

'Got a knife, Henson?' he asked. 'Something with a slim blade?'

'Uh-huh.'

'Go heat it over the fire.'

While Moore did as he was told, Cannon washed his hands thoroughly in the water provided, then used the scissors to cut the tunic and undershirt away from the wound. When it was revealed, it looked deceptively minor, just a small hole surrounded by faintly blue, puffy flesh.

Clenching his teeth, Cannon carefully pressed on the wound with the heel of his hand, maintaining the pressure until the bleeding had slowed to a lazy dribble. The wounded man stirred a little but didn't regain consciousness.

When Cannon looked up again he saw that the other two constables had returned to the cabin and were watching him with wide eyes in pale faces. He snapped, 'Make yourselves useful, you men. Come and hold his arms and legs, and hold him tight. When I dig for the bullet he's going to buck like a mustang. Henson?'

Moore came over and handed him the heated knife. It was a wooden-handled rabbiter's knife, about the best he could hope for in the circumstances. He took it, paused for one brief moment, then steeled himself and said, 'Hold him fast, now.'

The Mounties tightened their grip on their sergeant's wrists and ankles.

Cannon plunged the blade in the water. The blade was so hot that water beaded along its length and spat steam.

Then, using the thumb and forefinger of his left hand to hold the wound open, he inserted the blade as gently as he could.

The wounded man screamed and started thrashing around. It was all his men could do to hold him down. Doing his best to ignore them and concentrate on the job at hand, Cannon set his jaw and dug the blade a little deeper, and then a little deeper still until he felt the point scratch at something hard: the base of the bullet.

'Found it,' he murmured. 'Keep him still.'

Sweating now, he moved the blade to the edge of the deformed bullet, pushed it a little deeper to get leverage and then, teeth clamped hard, pulled back quickly.

The spent bullet popped out of the hole and with it came a great red spurt of blood. Cannon handed the knife to Moore, said, 'Clean it and heat it again,' and then once more covered the wound with the heel of his hand, applying pressure to stop the renewed flow of blood.

While he was doing it, he glanced down at the whiskey bottle. He could use a pull of that sneaky pete himself about now. But when he was finally satisfied that the bleeding had slowed again, all he did was take the bottle, tell the constables to hold their grip and then spill some of the liquor into the wound to clean it.

Again MacLeod twisted, squirmed and howled. Again it was all his men could do to stop him from wriggling right off the table. Cannon took a rag, quickly patted the wound dry, then called, 'Henson?'

Once again Moore appeared at his shoulder and handed him the re-heated blade. With barely a pause Cannon laid it flat against the wound, where it sizzled and burned. Only when he was satisfied that the wound had been closed and cauterized did he drop it into the bowl.

At last he allowed himself a generous

pull on the bottle. The whiskey burned right the way down into his belly and was probably the best drink he'd ever taken. He looked down at MacLeod and drank again, this time to the man's health. The Mountie had lapsed back into unconsciousness. There was little more that could be done for him now save bandage the wound, put him to bed somewhere and, if it was in your nature, pray like hell.

5

MacLeod survived the night, and that in itself was more than anyone had expected. Not only that, but he even found the strength to summon Cannon to the Mounties' bunkhouse behind the cabin a little after first light, there to thank him huskily for what he'd done.

Neither man mentioned Sweeney, and Cannon and the rest of the stampeders neither saw nor heard of him again.

Two days later they dropped down below the tree-line and out onto a broad slope that led toward the tent-town that had grown up around Lake Bennett, the final stopping-off point before Dawson City.

Lake Bennett was a narrow, miles-long stretch of still, icy blue water surrounded by sweeping, pine-timbered slopes and misty grey mountains. Its shores had been mulched by the passage of many boots and into the mud had been stamped a curly carpet of butter-coloured wood-shavings, for it was here that the stampeders had chosen to build the boats that would take them on the final leg of the journey up the Yukon River.

As they trudged closer, Cannon saw that thousands of adventurers had already pitched camp to await a break in the appalling weather. It was October right now, a month when the elements could be notoriously fickle, but from November through till April, winter would lock the land in its grip, and no-one wanted to be stranded here when that happened, not with the goldfields — which even now lay more than two hundred miles away — so tantalizingly close.

They spied a reasonably free area on the far side of the sprawling camp and headed for it, intending to establish their own temporary base there. Around them, the crowded tent city stank of soapsuds, coffee, sweat and burnt food, and the constant babble of voices carried with them the accents of Germany and Czechoslovakia, Great Britain, Australia, France and Canada itself.

They passed makeshift eateries, saloons and stores, even a rough-and-ready infirmary and a Presbyterian tent church outside which a preacher was addressing his small audience from atop an old tea chest.

Cannon spotted a long line of men carrying axes, saws and hatchets toward a stand of timber fifty yards away, and guessed — correctly, as it turned out — that they were going to cut trees for the rafts and boats they would need to negotiate the river.

This raised a new consideration, and once they'd established their camp he raised the subject with his companions. They could either build a boat or hire one of the experienced boatmen who'd already set up shop hereabouts to ferry them down to Dawson. The latter would be expensive, though, for the boatmen had long-since learned their value and didn't come cheap.

After some discussion, they took a vote and decided to build their own rough-and-ready flatboat.

Eager to reach journey's end now, Cannon spent the next week doing his bit and more with a borrowed axe. He felled pines, cleaned them down to the trunk, then dragged them to the water's edge, where some of their new-found friends, who knew about such matters, set to work with cross-cut saws and began to fashion the vessel.

Over the next few days the stampeders began to move out rather than risk being snowed in until April. Each new dawn saw men pack up their tents and supplies and carry their boats down to the edge of the lake. The mass exodus was finally underway.

By this time Cannon, Moore, Tyson and six other men from their original party had constructed a large, reasonably stable flatboat with a single canvas sail. They'd just finished lashing their supplies in the centre and were tying a canvas tent over them to protect them from the weather when a small, dark-complexioned man of about thirty came up to the water's edge and called, 'Ahoy, there! You fellers know what's up ahead, I take it?'

Cannon turned to face him. 'Some,' he replied cautiously. He'd heard plenty of talk, of course: a chain of lakes — Bennett, Nares, Tagish, Marsh and Laberge — leading down into the glacier-fed Yukon River, the journey punctuated along the way by deadly rapids at Miles Canyon, Whitehorse and Five Finger.

'Then you know it's gonna be a bitch,' the little man said bluntly. He waved one arm to indicate the crowded shores to either side of them. 'Fully half the men here won't make it, leastways not alive. But you will . . . if you hire me to guide you down to Dawson.'

'How much?'

The little pilot glanced at the raft and the nine men aboard. 'Call it an even three hundred.'

'Kind of overpriced, aren't you?'

'I can get you where you want to go, and I can get you there in one piece. Lord knows, I've done it often enough in the past. But if you'd sooner take your chances alone . . . '

Cannon glanced over one shoulder. 'What do you men think?'

Once again they deferred to Moore, who said, 'Pay him. He'll get us through, I reckon, an' he'll earn every penny doin' it.'

'All right,' said Cannon. 'You got yourself a deal.'

'Are you almost ready to go?' asked the little man.

'We are ready.'

'Then let's get to it,' said the other, throwing his own small sack of gear aboard and following it over the crude bulwark. 'Name's Landon, by the way. Bartholemew Landon.'

Many of the remaining stampeders were now taking to the water in large numbers, some in boats that looked more seaworthy than others. There were crude kayaks and canoes, flat-bottomed skiffs, scows, lighters, sharpies, outriggers, keelboats, rafts and sculls.

Landon took up a position at the bow and waited while Cannon and Tyson hoisted their single sail and adjusted it toward the rising wind. Then, shoving off with long poles of stripped wood, they drifted slowly away from the shore.

'Water's calm right now,' called Landon as they edged toward the middle of the lake. 'But when we come upon Miles Canyon the fun and games'll begin! So just make sure you keep your wits about you and do *what* I tell you, *when* I tell you, and we'll all live to a ripe old age.'

Taken by the wind, the boat continued to sail steadily in the wake of the vessels ahead of it, bobbing like a cork every time it hit the waves, and gradually its passengers began to trade grins, for this wasn't anywhere near as bad as they'd expected it to be.

Only Moore and Cannon knew better than to drop their guard.

Gradually the motley collection of craft spread out. Some overtook others, some began to take on water and quickly sank, their occupants being forced to swim and splutter back to shore. For the remainder, the journey along Lake Bennett was almost pleasant, if you ignored the biting wind and driving sleet.

Eventually the flatboat followed the leading vessels across shallow Nares Lake. Three miles on they entered Lake Tagish, with its mountainous shores, all seventeen miles of them studded with willow, spruce and poplar.

At last Tagish emptied out into Marsh Lake, and still the going was good.

But then they came to Miles Canyon.

The channel ahead narrowed between high walls of corrugated rock and began to twist from left to right and back again. Beside Landon, Tyson swallowed nervously and said, 'What's that noise up ahead? Th-thunder?'

'That's the rapids, my friend,' replied Landon.

Even as he spoke, they rounded a

bend in the canyon and up ahead the water began to froth with such ferocity that it looked more like boiling milk. As it was claimed by the current, the flatboat's speed started to increase and it veered a little sideways.

'Hold on tight!' called Landon, and Moore turned and gestured to the jumbled craft behind them that danger lay ahead.

A quarter-mile in front, one of the lighters had already fallen victim to the unpredictable current. Even as they watched, it rose up, then crashed down again with water exploding around it.

A moment later the lighter began to turn almost lazily as the rapids took control. The vessel turned sideways on and began to veer towards the left-side bank. The occupants of the flatboat could only watch as the lighter rammed into the bank with enough force to hurl the passengers off their feet. Then the churning water propelled the vessel on, but now it was holed and taking in freezing water, and there was panic aboard as it began to list and sink ever lower into the river.

Men fought to salvage their gear and splash madly for the thin strip of shore before the water stole away all the feeling in their arms and legs, but that was easier said than done, for there was a dangerous undercurrent here that quickly tore the heavy-laden swimmers away from their chosen course and dragged them under.

'Further left!' yelled Landon. 'Left now, and be sharp about it!'

Reuben Sykes, the man who had been given charge of the rudder, pushed to the right. Immediately, the flatboat, now topping and yawing, obeyed the command.

The boat rocked drunkenly as it shot across the rapids, and Cannon staggered across to give Sykes a hand to keep the vessel on course. White water burst up over the sides to drench the men clinging to the stacked supplies for safety.

They were moving at a bouncing,

dipping blur now, zipping past those
men still struggling desperately to reach
the shore, and the flatboat was shudder-
ing and shaking every time it crashed
into the flotsam that had so recently
been the lighter. The noise was
deafening, the rush and crash of white
water, the blood-chilling yells of drown-
ing men, the howl of the wind as it
ripped through the canyon and threatened to tear down their sail.

'Now sharp to the right!' bawled Landon,
himself soaked by spray. 'Straight onto
the rocks now, fellows! Straight, I said!'

Cannon frowned, wondering if their
pilot had taken leave of his senses.
Sykes was entertaining similar doubts,
because he hauled the rudder in the
opposite direction.

'Head for the rocks!' yelled Landon.

He'd told them he was no stranger to
this job, but had he lied just to get his
hands on their money? It was hardly
likely that he'd risk his own life as well
as theirs . . . wasn't it?

Reaching a decision, Cannon pulled

the rudder back, out of Sykes' grip, and the flatboat sped like an Indian arrow across the boiling water toward the rocks Landon had indicated.

Before he could grab the rudder again, Sykes slipped, fell and slid across the deck to fetch up hard against the starboard bulwark. Cannon was left to fight the restless rudder alone. He shot Tyson a look. The boy's face was greener than a meadow in May, but he got the message and staggered to the stern to lend a hand.

They skimmed on across the turbulent surface, still rising high and then crashing forward again, but the flatboat held together and continued to take the pounding.

Ahead of them another boat had fallen foul of the treacherous waters. Caught in their grip, an outrigger that had looked flimsy to begin with suddenly began to spin in circles and then snap apart. Her two-man crew grabbed their gear and leapt into the water, then struck out for shore. Behind them, their boat tipped up and fell apart like matchwood.

Without warning the flatboat slammed into some hidden underwater obstruction, maybe the wreck of a boat that had come down the rapids a day or two before. For an instant it seemed to shiver and somehow distort, then righted itself and continued on. Water flowed around their ankles, and a couple of the stampeders made clumsy attempts to bail them out with their cupped hands. Another lost his footing, struck his head and was now trying to stem the flow of blood with a sodden rag.

Still fighting the rudder and obeying Landon's every command, Cannon heard Tyson say something and yelled, 'What was that?'

The youngster's face was pebbled with freezing spray, and his eyes were closed down to slits against the buffeting wind. 'I said we're not going to make it, are w — ?'

They hit another obstruction, the flatboat shook violently and everyone was thrown to the deck, but still the vessel continued to leap and crash through the white-tops with Landon, now clinging white-knuckled to the bow and drenched to the skin, still shouting directions.

Cannon scrambled back up, grabbed the rudder, set himself as best he could and kept following orders, and a few turbulent minutes later they left the raging waters behind them.

At last their speed decreased, and though wind still filled their sail, it no longer threatened to rip it free. Men picked themselves up, checked for broken bones and then heaved sighs of relief, and watching them, Landon surprised everyone by allowing himself a hearty chuckle.

'Everyone all right?' he called.

There came weary nods and murmurs of assent.

'Good,' said their pilot. 'Because when we reach Whitehorse, which should be any time now, we've got to do this whole damn' thing all over again!'

6

Landon was right. They went through it all over again at Whitehorse, where hidden boulders almost ripped the bottom out of the flatboat, and once more at Five Finger, and in between the two they had to endure a choppy crossing of windswept Lake Laberge. Only when they finally came to Thirty Mile and joined the sluggish yellow waters of the Yukon did things turn a little more peaceful.

Allowing for delays — minor injuries, repairs to the boat, holing up during the worst storms — the journey took five days and four nights. Even after what passed for dark at this latitude, the sun never dropped below the horizon, so they were able to keep moving as long as Landon considered it safe to do so.

Still, the mood of the stampeders was noticeably quieter now. This final stage of the journey had tested them to the full, and found all too many wanting. While crimson twilight hung between the trees, Cannon and his companions spent their evenings drying off their wet clothes and remembering the men who had set sail alongside them at Lake Bennett and died en route or came close to it. Even now a number were fighting losing battles with their chills.

What was left of the mismatched fleet set sail early on the morning of the fifth day, and as Landon had predicted, the going now became, if not exactly easier, then at least a little less difficult than it had been.

It was a little after noon and Cannon was forrard, huddling against the cold and thinking as always about Beth and Amy, when he heard Tyson murmur, 'I think I'm dreamin'.'

He glanced over at the youngster. 'What was that, Jeff?'

Tyson gave no sign that he'd heard the question. His eyes were fixed almost wonderingly on the river ahead.

Cannon turned and followed his gaze. About two hundred yards away, the waterway split in two. This, he figured, must be the confluence of the Yukon and Klondike Rivers.

Which meant . . .

As the flatboat rounded a gentle curve, so the western shore hove into sight . . . a shore beyond which rose an untidy cluster of tents, shacks, shanties and larger structures — a lot of them.

'Dawson City,' muttered Tyson. And then, louder, '*Dawson City!*'

Tyson's cry galvanized everyone, and was quickly taken up by his companions and those fetching up in the vessels fore and aft. Pistols were produced, both by the men afloat and those watchers ashore, and discharged into the cobalt sky.

Dipping oars or trimming sails, the newcomers closed the distance as fast as they could.

'We made it, Mr Cannon!' Tyson grinned, and there were tears in his eyes. 'We made it, by God! Now I can start digging for gold — an' make my Susan the richest woman on the planet!'

★ ★ ★

Dawson, the so-called Pearl of the North, was packed solid. Every spare lot had been filled, either with tent stores and saloons or hastily-constructed cabins, shacks and grander, false-fronted business establishments. As they drew closer, crowds began to gather along the shore to watch their arrival.

As the flatboat glided toward shore, men came splashing down into the muddy shallows to help drag the vessel the last few yards. There were yelled greetings and hearty handshakes all round, after which Cannon, Moore, Tyson and the others collected their gear and stamped stiffly ashore.

For a while longer all was chaos, but after paying Landon and saying their goodbyes to the men who'd travelled with them all the way from Dyea, the three companions walked wearily up into the city itself.

By any stretch of the imagination, Dawson was a marvel, and it was hard to believe that it had only been in existence for ten months. Main Street was a wide, muddy thoroughfare along which just about every business you could think of stood shoulder-to-shoulder with its neighbour. And it was just as well they did, because frost had damaged the foundations of each, which in turn had caused every solid structure there to bend, lean and buckle and give the place a weird, old-before-its-time appearance.

After spending so long in the wilderness, the hustle and bustle took some adjusting to, and all at once the long journey caught up with Cannon. He was here at last, in the closest thing to civilization he was likely to find in this ass-end of the world. But right now all he craved was good food and decent whiskey and a long, dreamless sleep in a warm feather bed. Emmet Lawrence had waited this long: Cannon figured he could wait one more day.

'Come on, fellers,' he said, brightening suddenly. 'My treat.'

Moore frowned. 'How's that again?'

Instead of answering him, Cannon led them across the street to a large, worn-canvas tent outside which a shingle proclaimed hot baths for five dollars a time. Inside, a dozen battered tin tubs were lined up in three rows, and water was heating in pots suspended over four large fires, which made the soap-scented air warm and comfortable. Cannon paid for three baths, and when they became available he and his companions shucked their gear and stripped off, Tyson with the blushing self-consciousness of youth.

Still, he forgot his inhibitions as soon as he lowered himself into the water. No words could describe just how good it felt. It warmed blood that had been chilled too often and eased muscles that felt as if they'd done more work in the last two months than they had in the last two years. Each man soaked in grateful silence, until Cannon and Tyson finally broke out their shaving tackle and set about scraping the whiskers off their chins.

Afterwards, having changed into clean clothes and left their old ones for laundering, they stopped by a barbershop and completed their transformations with a haircut each, then went into a crowded saloon and toasted each other and the memories of all the men who hadn't made it. Finally they went to an eatery — extortionately overpriced, like everything else in Dawson — and Cannon stood them a passable meal of chicken, dumplings and canned beans.

The afternoon was just starting to wane by the time they stepped back out onto the uneven boardwalk and looked at each other for possibly the last time. Goodbyes were seldom easy, especially for men whose friendship had been forged over a long period of adversity, and these weren't going to be any exception.

Moore said, 'Why don't you stick with us, Tom? I reckon we three could make a mighty successful trio.'

'I reckon we could at that,' Cannon agreed. 'But I've already got a job, remember?'

'Finding your missing man,' said Moore. 'Well, I wish you luck with it.'

'And to you, my friends,' said Cannon, grasping first with Moore, then Tyson.

The old man and his young companion gathered up their gear and started down off the boardwalk, intending to buy additional supplies before going in search of a claim to stake, but as they did so a flatbed wagon came hurtling along the centre of the street, the driver, perched high on his seat, cracking a long, thin whip over the heads of his two-horse team.

Men, women and horseback riders scattered before him. Two women who'd been struggling to cross the swampy street and not soil the hems of their dresses had to dash out of his way or risk being trampled. Even so, the horses' pounding hoofs and the wagon's blurring wheels splashed them with slush as it rattled past.

Moore shook his head and said, 'Crazy galoot.'

Even as he spoke, the wagon's wheels lost their purchase on the muddy ground and the back of the vehicle started fish-tailing wildly. Cannon snapped, 'Get back up here, Henson.'

Before the old man could react, the wagon slewed dangerously to the left and clipped him as it rattled by. Moore was spun violently and flung to the wet ground in its wake. Tyson's eyes widened and he cried, 'Greybeard!'

As the wagon continued up the street, Cannon dropped his gear and hurried to Moore's aid. The old man's face was screwed up in pain and he was clutching his right arm.

'Henson! You all right?'

It was several moments before Moore could speak. At last he rasped, 'Think I've . . . busted my arm.'

Cannon's mouth tightened. The way the arm was hanging, the shoulder had certainly been dislocated.

Concerned and curious townsfolk gathered around them as Cannon and Tyson helped Moore to his feet and carried him back into the eatery. As the old man sat down, he winced and shuddered at the pain of his injury.

'That's the trouble with old bones,' he muttered. 'They get real brittle.' He glanced up at his companions and forced a fleeting smile that didn't quite reach his pain-filled eyes. 'I sure hope that sonofabitch had good reason to be drivin' like a madman.'

'Don't bank on it,' said the restaurant owner, who'd seen what had happened and now hurried over with a mug of whiskey-laced coffee for the pale-faced victim. 'That's Tim Fletcher, mister, an' he's a law unto himself.'

'Is he, now?' said Cannon, the sight of his injured friend bringing with it a sudden, uncharacteristic stab of anger. To the owner he said, 'Keep an eye on my gear for a while?'

'Sure.'

'Thanks. Jeff?'

'Sir?'

'Get Henson to a sawbones soon as you can.'

'Sure. Where're you going?'

'To see a man about a wagon.'

He pushed back through the crowd and out onto the street. The wagon, he saw, was standing in front of the saloon at which they'd recently been drinking, about fifty yards away. The knowledge only stoked his anger. The only hurry Tim Fletcher had been in was to get to the nearest watering-hole.

He stepped down into the street, crossed to the opposite boardwalk and headed for the saloon, which was a large, single room with a low tin ceiling, a long plank-and-barrel counter along the left-hand wall and a loose-boarded floor covered with sawdust, across which was scattered a few mismatched tables.

The man Cannon was after was

standing at the near end of the counter, throwing the contents of a shot glass back in a single swallow, much to the approval of the handful of comrades surrounding him. He was tall and thickset, about thirty-five, with a thick, greasy beard the colour of coal.

Mouth tight, Cannon pushed in beside him, set an elbow on the bar, turned to him and, after a pause, slowly waved his free palm before the man's face.

Fletcher stopped drinking and fixed him with a belligerent glare. He had pocked skin and a flat, once-broken nose that was now little more than a raddled knob of flesh between heavy-lidded brown eyes. 'What the hell you think you're doin', mister?' he growled, his voice sounding more like an ominous shifting of loose gravel.

'Just checking to make sure your eyes work,' replied Cannon.

'Huh?'

'I figured you must be blind, the way you were driving your wagon just now.'

At last understanding dawned, and Fletcher's cool smile revealed big yellow teeth. He was bundled up in a heavy wool coat and duck pants tucked into stovepipe boots, and beneath a high-crowned fur hat with a four-inch brim, he appeared to be as bald as an egg.

'You're talkin' about them two whores tried to cross my path just now,' he said.

'Those and the old man whose arm you just broke.'

Fletcher shrugged. 'Well, I don't know nothin' about an old man, but I can tell you this, *cheechako*. The folks who don't step wide around me get trampled. Remember that yourself. You'll live longer.'

Using the scarred fist curled around his empty shot glass, he pushed Cannon hard in the chest. 'Now take a hike,' he said. 'I've just hit colour an' I got some celebratin' to do.'

Encouraged by the laughter of his cronies, Fletcher pushed him again: the second push that Cannon allowed no man.

'All right,' he replied with a nod. 'You've had your say, big man. Now you heed *this*.'

No sooner had the last word left his lips than he treated Fletcher to a bone-smashing blow to the jaw, and Fletcher tottered backward, more in surprise than anything else. Even as he yelled a curse, Cannon followed up with a roundhouse right, a left, then another right, and Fletcher's hat went flying, revealing his hairless head.

As startled drinkers hastily cleared a space for them, the saloon exploded with the sound of yelling and cheering, but Cannon was only dimly aware of it. His attention was focused on Fletcher, and with good reason. The combination of blows would have put any other man down, but Fletcher was still on his feet. Not only that — he was also roaring back into the fray with his own fists swinging.

All at once it was Cannon's turn to

retreat. He blocked the first blow but caught the second on his freshly-shaved jaw. Pain exploded through him, for Fletcher was a big man and the blow carried better than two hundred pounds behind it, and he lost his own curl-brimmed Stetson.

He blocked another punch that numbed his arm, and then one more, but still Fletcher came surging after him like a runaway locomotive. The big man brought a knee up with the intention of mashing Cannon's crotch, but Cannon swerved, the knee missed, and while Fletcher was off-balance he powered back in and caught him with a fist that sank wrist-deep into Fletcher's gut.

Fletcher's mouth fell open. Stale breath hit Cannon in a noisy gust. Sickened by it, he hit Fletcher another right cross to the jaw, a left, right, left, and then Fletcher grabbed him, lifted him off his feet and threw him at the bar, and Cannon slammed down onto the rough-hewn boards, scattering bottles and glasses in every direction before disappearing over the far side.

Still roaring, Fletcher ran to the bar, reached over to get his hands on his opponent and finish the job once and for all, but Cannon had other ideas. Down on all fours, he came out through a gap between two barrels, grabbed Fletcher by his booted ankles and yanked hard, and Fletcher crashed over onto his back.

Cannon scrambled out after him, leapt on him, grabbed him by the ears and cracked his bald head against the floorboards once, then again. Fletcher twisted, threw him off, and then it was a race to see which of them could regain his feet first.

Winded and aching, each man managed to get as far as his knees, and then Cannon clubbed Fletcher with all the strength he had left, and the bigger man went down like a felled redwood and lay there, bleeding from the mouth, from a cut over his brow, gasping for air and struggling to remain conscious.

However, it was a struggle he couldn't

hope to win, and at last, as he finally gave it up, the saloon went wild. Though Fletcher had friends in the crowd, Cannon was clearly a popular winner. Somehow he regained his feet and went in search of his hat, knowing he shouldn't have given in to his temper but feeling better because he knew he'd evened the score a little for Moore.

He flexed his fingers to ease the stringing in them, clapped his hat back onto his pounding head and, breathing hard, headed for the doors.

He'd gone maybe three steps when someone yelled, 'Look out!'

Cannon spun back immediately, right hand blurring inside his jacket to close around the butt of his Colt. Fletcher, he saw, had managed to sit up and haul out a pistol of his own, which he was even now bringing up to line.

In almost the same instant, however, a shotgun blast slammed through the smoky confines of the saloon, deafening everyone, and the boards between Fletcher's splayed legs suddenly exploded in a shower of spinters. The miner yelped like a woman, quickly threw the gun aside and raised his rough hands high.

With the man no longer a threat, Cannon released his trapped breath, allowed his stomach to uncoil and left the Colt in leather. Glancing around, he saw that the man who'd fired the shot and in all probability saved him from an early grave was standing just inside the doorway, a long-barrelled shotgun held in his gloved hands. He was a runty little bantam just over five and a half feet tall, with a small, pinched, sour-looking face that was shadowed by the brim of a large black hat. He was forty-ish, pale, dressed in a dark sack coat buttoned to the throat, and well-cut cowskin boots. Pinned to his coat was a shield upon which had been engraved the words DEPUTY SHERIFF.

'What's all this about?' he barked, coming two paces closer.

One of the men in the crowd, clearly a crony of Fletcher's, stabbed a finger at Cannon and said, 'He jus' came in an' started swingin', Bob! Di'n't give Tim no chance at all!'

The deputy's black, button-bright eyes settled on Cannon's battered face. 'That right, mister?'

Cannon said, 'He came into town aboard a wagon. It's parked outside. He was driving it too fast and he nearly hit a couple of women. He did hit a friend of mine, an old man. Busted his arm.'

'So you figured you'd teach him a lesson, is that it?'

'Pretty much.'

'Got a name, have you?'

Cannon told him what it was, adding, 'Good job for me you showed up when you did.'

The deputy shrugged. 'Any time I hear a ruckus as loud as the one I heard comin' from this place, I know there's mischief afoot.' Looking at Fletcher he said, 'An' I usually guess who's behind it. Want to press charges, Cannon? Attempted murder's a good place to start.'

Cannon shook his head.

'All right,' said the deputy. 'Be on your way, Tim, an' don't show your ugly mug in Dawson again for a good long while. You too, Cannon. Las' thing we need in this town is another troublemaker.'

'I'm not a troublemaker.'

'Well, you sure got the look of one.'

Cannon managed a grin. 'I can't help that. But if you're so anxious to see the back of me, maybe you can give me some help that'll get me out of here all the sooner.'

'How so?'

Cannon glanced around. 'It's not a long story, but it's a private one. All right if I stop by your office later on?'

'Sure,' said the deputy. 'Just ask for Bob Evers. Anyone'll give you directions.'

7

When Cannon got back to the eatery and retrieved his gear, the owner of the place told him he'd sent Moore and Tyson along to Doc Neuberger's office as soon as Moore felt able to walk, then told him how to get there. By the time he reached the doctor's surgery — a narrow, draughty shack occupying space between a meat market and a livery stable — Moore had been shot full of laudanum, his shoulder had been re-located and his broken arm set. Now the old man was recovering in a creaky ladderback chair beside the door, looking pasty-white and drained. The doctor, meanwhile, was on the other side of the room, fumbling around with a none-too-clean set of pliers as he tried to extract a bad tooth from his next wriggling patient.

'Been frettin' about you,' Moore husked when Cannon finally came inside. He ran his drugged eyes across Cannon's battered face and added, 'With good reason, by the looks.'

Before Cannon could do more than nod a greeting to Tyson, the doctor glanced around and said, 'Be right with you, mister.'

'It's OK, Doc. I'm not a customer.'

'Then why the hell you clutterin' up my office?'

''Cause he's a friend o' mine,' snapped Moore, some of his old fire returning briefly. He shook his head at Cannon and said, 'I swear, Tom, if this feller really is a doctor, I guess that makes me a Chinese acrobat.'

'I heard that, you old buzzard.'

'You were *meant* to, Doc. Still, he fixed me up, after a fashion, so I guess I can't complain.'

'You've done all right so far,' snarled the doctor, still struggling to get a grip on the slippery molar.

'You ready to move?' asked Cannon.

'Nope,' replied Moore. 'But I reckon I've worn out my welcome around here, so I guess we'd better.'

'You've got *that* right,' called the doctor, but he was smiling as he said it.

Tyson helped the old man to his feet and they all left together. Outside, Cannon said, 'You know you'll have to rest up a while, Henson, give that wing of yours a chance to heal.'

'It'll set us back, an' that's a fact,' sighed the old-timer. Glancing at Tyson he said, 'You might want to consider goin' it alone from here on out, button. State I'm in right now, I'll only slow you down.'

But Tyson shook his head. 'Don't bank on it,' he replied. 'I reckon I can do the work of two till you're strong enough to pull your weight again, Greybeard. 'Sides, you've watched out for me ever since we left San Francisco. Now I figure it's my turn to watch out for you.'

Hearing that, Moore made a fidgety, embarrassed gesture and quickly glanced down at his boots. 'You're both good boys,' he said thickly. 'Man couldn't want for better friends.'

With their plans changed, leastways for the moment, and Moore almost dead on his feet from the powerful opiate, they decided to accompany Cannon to the first hotel that wasn't packed to the seams, and allow him to book them into the last two rooms available. Since Moore and Tyson were happy to share, Cannon was able to enjoy the first real privacy he'd known since leaving Frisco.

Promising to see his companions again in the morning, he threw his gear into the wardrobe, bathed his aching face in the chipped chamber set on the dresser, then locked the door behind him and went in search of the deputy marshal.

The sky was darkening now, leastways about as much as it was likely to darken this far north, but around him Dawson seemed as lively as ever. The first person he stopped gave him directions to the deputy's office, and he found it ten minutes later. A blocky, flat-roofed structure built from reclaimed clinker bricks, with a heavy wooden door and small windows that were shuttered and barred, it was little more than a satellite office designed to handle all the trouble in this particular part of town — and if the sizeable crowd of miners who'd gathered outside was anything to go by, trouble had already arrived.

'What's happening, friend?' he asked as he drew to a halt on the fringe of the gathering.

'That depends on Evers,' growled a short man with a pocked nose and a thick beard. Some of the men were carrying burning torches, and they threw an amber radiance over the scene. 'If he takes us serious an' does somethin' about it, that'll be an end to it. But if he keeps sittin' on the fence or turnin' a blind eye, we'll damn'-well handle it ourselves!'

'Handle what?'

Before the little man could answer, the law office door opened and two tough-looking men, presumably the crowd's spokesmen, came out onto the board-walk, followed by the deputy sheriff. At

117

once the crowd came roaring to life.

'Well?'

'Yeah, what's he say, Joe?'

'It had better be good!'

'He'd better — '

'Pipe down!' bawled Evers, facing them head-on, his jaw muscles bunching as the orange-grey shadows danced across his narrow face. 'I've heard what you men've had to say, an' I've given my assurance that I'll do as much as I can about it!'

Immediately there was another round of hoots and cat-calls. Whatever the problem was, the miners clearly had little faith in Evers to sort it out.

'I can't do more'n that!' he yelled over the clamour. 'But I tell you what I can do — I can arrest you men if you don't move along, an' charge you with disturbin' the peace! I'll do it too, you know I will! Now go on, break it up, an' leave it to me! I'll see Bleeker in the mornin' an' give it to him straight!'

'An' you think Bleeker'll listen to you?' called someone in the crowd.

'He'd better,' Evers replied. 'I'm the law.'

He sounded determined enough, but as he ran his bright, black-button eyes over the crowd, he could see that he still hadn't won them over.

'Now move along,' he advised. 'An' I'll tell you what I've just told Joe and Ezra here — don't get any ideas about takin' matters into your own hands! Bleeker's done nothing illegal — '

'Nothin' you care to acknowledge!' someone called back.

'He's done nothin' illegal,' Evers continued grimly. 'An' until he does, the best I can do is try to reason with him.'

'You can't reason with a bastard like that!'

'Well, at least give me the chance to try.'

That, at least, was a reasonable request, and one of the two spokesmen raised his big, dirty hands for calm. 'We'll do like he says!' he announced, his voice a deep baritone. 'But now I'll tell *you* somethin', Evers. You go on an' have your word with Bleeker. But if he still won't change his ways, we'll deal with him ourselves, an' the law be damned!'

Evers turned on him. 'For your sake, Joe,' he growled, 'I'll pretend I didn't hear that.'

The two spokesmen hopped down off the boardwalk and the thirty-strong crowd fell into step behind them. Cannon stayed where he was, watching them go. Up on the boardwalk the deputy did likewise.

'Trouble?' Cannon asked after a moment.

Evers peered down at him, frowning briefly until recognition dawned. 'Cannon, right?'

'Right.'

'There's always trouble in this damn' town, Cannon,' he replied. He ran a hand up through his short-cut mouse-brown hair. 'Better come inside.'

The single lamp-lit room on the far side of the heavy door was split in two by the bars of a large communal cell. One dark-haired man, the cell's only occupant, was curled up asleep on the scarred bench that ran the length of the back wall.

The office half of the building was a little more welcoming. A small wood stove sat against the facing wall, its doors open to reveal the fire inside. Facing the stove sat the deputy's large desk, to which Evers now retreated.

'So, Mr Cannon,' he said tiredly. 'How is it you think I can help you?'

'I'm looking for a man.'

Evers gave him a look. 'Business or personal?'

'Business.'

'You the law where you come from?'

'No.'

'Bounty hawk?'

'No. This man, Emmet Lawrence, came north little over a while ago to seek his fortune, but somewhere along the way his letters stopped coming and his wife hired me to find out what became of him.'

Evers offered a mirthless chuckle. 'Well, I sure wish you luck with that,' he said drily. 'You got any idea just how many men we got in this city?'

'Some.'

'Then what does a name like 'Emmet Lawrence' mean to the likes of me, or even a description, if it comes to that? Any case, this man's story's no different to a hundred others I've heard — a hundred this week alone! They come to get rich quick, they disappear. You've made the same journey he made, so you know the score. This Lawrence could've met his fate in any one of a dozen different ways 'twixt San Francisco and here. He might even have taken up with an Indian woman an' decided to forget all about the one he left behind! Some of these Tlingit women, they're better than they sound, you know.'

Cannon nodded. Evers wasn't telling him anything he didn't already know. His chances of finding Lawrence were slim at best. But he'd bucked odds like that before.

'I know for sure he made it this far,' he replied. 'He wrote and told his wife all about Dawson. Then the letters stopped coming.' Reaching into his pocket, he brought out the daguerreotype Lorna Lawrence had given him and passed it across. 'This is what he looked like before he set sail.'

Evers studied the picture for a while. Finally he handed it back. 'If I ever met him, I don't recall it.'

'Too bad.'

The deputy eyed him curiously. 'What's this wife of his paying you to find him, anyway?' he asked. 'Must be a fair piece, to make a man come all this way.'

'It's enough,' Cannon replied softly.

'What was he, then? Before he came north, I mean. Businessman?'

'Not really. He married into money, but didn't care much for being kept. He figured it should be the man who keeps the woman, not the other way around.'

'Shame it didn't work out for him.'

'Well, we don't know that yet, leastways not for sure. You got a newspaper in this town, Deputy?'

'The Klondike *Nugget*.'

'Maybe I'll ask around there. You never know, someone might remember him, or what became of him.'

'Check the obituaries first,' Evers suggested bleakly. 'You might find him quicker that way.'

As he watched Cannon cross back to the door he called, 'If I turn anything up, where can I find you?'

'The Miner's Rest. Room seven.'

He went back out into the night.

* * *

A little after dawn the following morning he came awake to the telltale creak of a loose floorboard in the hallway outside, and instinctively reached for the Colt on the bedside table.

A second later there came a soft rapping at the door.

He swung out of bed, knowing that his visitor was probably Moore or Tyson or both, but there was always the chance that it might be Tim Fletcher instead, or one of his cronies, come to get even following yesterday's fight.

Standing to one side of the door he called quietly, 'Who is it?'

There was a brief hesitation. Then: 'Name won't mean squat to you. But if your name's Cannon, we need to talk.'

'Do we, now?'

'Yup,' said the voice, and then it added, 'About Emmet Lawrence.'

It occurred to him then that maybe Deputy Evers had been as good as his word, had asked around and actually turned something up. 'Hold on,' he said, and quickly slipped into his pants before unlocking the door.

The man standing outside was a large, heavyset half-breed Tlingit Indian. He raised his big hands when he saw the Colt in Cannon's fist and said, 'Whoa, there, mister. No call for that.'

Figuring that his visitor was probably right, Cannon pointed the gun floor-ward, but didn't put it away. 'Come in.'

The big 'breed did so. He had a wide, coffee-coloured face and hair that fell in a dusty black spill to his broad shoulders. He wore a wide-brimmed hat made out of spruce roots and a grubby poncho woven from goat hair. He was about thirty-five or so, but the cropped goatee beard shading his chin made him look older. His grass-green eyes, however, were a jarring contrast to his otherwise Indian heritage.

'So,' said Cannon, crossing to the window to pull the curtain and let the watery sunrise in. 'What do you know about Lawrence?'

'I know you're lookin' for him.'

'And . . . ?'

'An' I can take you straight to him. But it'll cost you.'

'I figured that. How much?'

'A thousand dollars. An' before you tell me you can't afford it, I already know that Lawrence's woman's got money to burn.'

'Who told you that?'

'You did,' grinned the half-breed. 'Last night.'

Something suddenly became clear to

him, and he stuffed the Colt into his waistband. 'You're the man I saw in Evers' cell. I thought you were asleep.'

'I was, till them riled-up miners showed up an' started shouting the odds about Bleeker. Who could sleep after that?'

'So you pretended . . . and eavesdropped instead.'

'Well, to tell it straight, I wasn't much interested in what you had to say till you mentioned Lawrence's name. Then I took notice.'

'And came here as soon as Evers cut you loose this morning?'

'More or less.'

'All right. About Lawrence. You know him?'

'Worked for him a time or two. I work for all the *cheechakos* some time or other. Helped him build his dugout.'

'What's he look like?'

'Tall, thin.'

Cannon snorted. 'I need more than that.'

'Dark hair, long face, beard.'

'Is this the man?' asked Cannon, showing him the daguerreotype.

The 'breed looked at it. 'That's him,' he confirmed. ' 'Course, he's lost a little weight since this was taken, his hair's longer an' like I say, he's grown a beard. But the eyes . . . the eyes're the same.'

'Where is he?' asked Cannon.

'That's what I'm selling.'

'All right,' Cannon replied. 'I'll buy it. For two hundred.'

The Tlingit shook his head. 'Five.'

'Three.'

'Four-fifty.'

'Four. And you don't get a red cent until I see Lawrence for myself.'

'Fair enough. He works a small claim no more'n ten miles from here.'

The 'breed wasn't telling him much. There were hundreds of claims within a ten-mile radius of Dawson. If he was on the level, it would take Cannon until well into the New Year to check every one himself.

'What do they call you, mister?' he asked after a moment's thought.

'Natuk.'

'Got a horse, Natuk?'

'Nope.'

'You know Doc Neuberger's surgery?'

'Yup.'

'There's a livery stable right next door. I'll meet you there in about an hour. We'll rent a couple of horses and you can take me right to Lawrence.'

Natuk nodded. 'I'll be there, mister. Sooner I hook you up with Lawrence, the sooner I get my money.'

*   *   *

As they left town a great blanket of low, slate-grey cloud drifted in to block out the sun, and it began to snow lightly. Cannon tucked his chin a little deeper into the buttoned collar of his lamb-leather jacket and closed the gloved fingers of his right hand firmer around the Winchester lever-action shotgun resting across his lap.

After the 'breed had let himself out, he'd washed and finished dressing, all the while wondering about Natuk and the story he'd told. Lawrence's letters had made no mention of a claim, small or otherwise, but perhaps he'd been hoping to surprise his wife with his success, or maybe he'd simply decided to say as little as possible in case his letters were intercepted.

Over a hasty breakfast with his companions, Moore in particular made no secret of his misgivings.

'Well, it all sounds a mite suspicious to me,' he said after Cannon finished telling them about the Tlingit's visit. 'Still, stranger things've happened. I saw a man cough up a bent nail once. Said he'd swallowed it for a bet thirty years earlier.' He shrugged carefully in order to favour his broken arm. 'Still, they's only one way to find out whether or not this Indian's tellin' it straight. You got to take him at his word till you know otherwise.'

'Why don't I ride along with you?' suggested Tyson. 'I know I probably wouldn't be much help in a fight, but it's like Greybeard always says: there's safety in numbers.'

'I appreciate the offer, Jeff, but I'll go alone.'

Natuk was waiting for him when he reached the livery stable. There was no missing the shotgun in Cannon's hands, and the half-breed eyed the weapon with clear respect. 'You're a cautious man, Mr Cannon,' he said.

Cannon nodded. 'Remember that.'

They rented horses and tack and set out fifteen minutes later, Cannon electing to ride behind his guide, not alongside him. As the snow-mantled country opened up ahead, the Tlingit called back, 'You don't trust me much, do you?'

'I don't trust you at all,' Cannon corrected.

'Well, you're not the only one leery of strangers,' Natuk said conversationally. 'Lawrence is funny that way, too. Don't trust too many people, and certainly not folks he's never met before. He'll never see you lessen I vouch for you first, so when we get close to where we're headed, I'll ride in ahead an' sort of pave the way, all right?'

'All right.'

He led them into and through a dense belt of quaking aspen, their leaves still resplendent with the rich reds, golds and yellows of the autumn just gone. Around them, another buffeting gust of cold wind made the occasional cluster of dwarf shrubs and fireweed tremble and sway.

'Does Lawrence work this claim of his alone?' called Cannon.

'Alone,' the 'breed replied over one shoulder.

The trees finally thinned and the trail ahead forked in two directions, both of them trending up toward a series of ridges topped by black spruce, poplars and, unusual for these parts, even the occasional birch. Natuk took the left-hand trail. Around them, the wind-driven snow continued to fall lightly.

Cannon carefully scanned their bleak surroundings. He figured they'd come about two miles from Dawson by now, and if Natuk meant him any harm, he'd make his play soon, for there was little point in leading him any further unless he really was on the level.

A small flock of grey jays erupted from a stand of spruce up ahead and to the left of the trail. Cannon wondered what, if anything, he should read into it. He'd had the feeling that he was being watched ever since they'd left Dawson, and though it was probably nothing more than a feeling, it persisted . . . and he knew better than to ignore it.

As they closed on the summit, the 'breed started chattering more freely, about the lousy weather, the high cost of whiskey, the hard bench he'd had to sleep on in Bob Evers' cell. He was trying to distract Cannon from thinking too much about their lonely surroundings, and who might be up there in the trees, waiting for them.

The timber came closer. Natuk pulled ahead ever so slightly. Getting out of the line of fire? Cannon was now almost certain of it.

Just as they drew parallel with the snow-heavy trees a sound carried to him on the cold wind: the small but unmistakable ching of a bridle chain. He knew then beyond all doubt that someone was in there, waiting for them, and that they meant him harm, that they were in cahoots with Natuk and that this had been the plan all along: to lead him to this lonely spot and then gun him down and rob him.

He saw by the sudden squaring of Natuk's shoulders that he'd heard the sound too, and was wondering if Cannon had recognized it for what it was. Deciding that he probably had, he did something with his reins that made his horse shy and sidestep a little: another diversionary tactic.

'Straighten up there, you mangy critter,' he told the horse, pretending to try and get it to do just that.

And at the same moment someone stepped out onto the trail behind them and yelled, 'Get you' hands up, you sonofabitch!'

8

Even before the newcomer finished yelling, Natuk spun his mount around and ripped a Remington single-action army revolver out from under his goat-hair poncho. 'Do like he — !'

Cannon shot him dead.

The instant before Natuk's chest vanished in a red mist, Cannon saw the man's green eyes go wide. Then the shotgun's ten-gauge blast punched him backwards off his startled horse and he landed heavily in the packed snow piled high beside the trail.

Even as the snow under him started streaking red, Cannon hauled on the reins to bring his own mount around to face Natuk's buddy. The man was standing splay-legged in the centre of the trail about ten yards away. He was a short, skinny Tlingit dressed in a dark blanket mackinaw and buckskin pants, with a disreputable straw topper pulled low over his forehead. He was still yelling, but his voice was breaking now, with the shock of having just seen Natuk die.

Cannon's horse reared up as he tried to draw a bead on his opponent. The man was holding a Model 1873 Winchester carbine in his hands: now he slapped the stock to one whiskery cheek and squeezed the trigger.

His bullet caught Cannon's horse in the chest, and the animal coughed, shuddered and then slammed over sideways, and Cannon had to kick free of his stirrups or have his leg crushed beneath it.

As he smashed into the snow, Natuk's buddy worked the lever and fired again. The bullet whined spitefully close but drilled harmlessly into a nearby drift.

Cannon came up on one knee, snap-aimed and fired the shotgun a second time. It made a sound like the end of the world and Straw Topper, realizing that this had all gone too badly wrong to be salvaged, turned and started running for the trees and, no doubt, his waiting horse.

Cannon yelled, 'Hold it!'

At the sound of his voice the man broke stride and whirled again, levering and firing from the hip over and over again, all the while still screaming.

Cannon levered too, and fired the shotgun a third time, smashing Straw Topper in the chest, plumb centre. The man flung his arms up and stumbled backwards, then turned and collapsed onto his side.

As the echoes of the gunshots died away and the howling of the wind came rushing back in to replace them, Cannon drew down a breath and scanned the trees until he was sure they held no more surprises. Only then did he finally allow himself to sag.

He looked from Natuk to his companion. They were already covered in a fine shroud of snow. He'd been right, then. The 'breed and his friend had been out to rob him.

But what if this business wasn't quite so clear-cut? What if Natuk had been telling it true, that he *had* known Lawrence, and that Lawrence had paid him to make sure his hunt for the man ended right here?

Pushing to his feet, he *shushed* over to Natuk and quickly checked his pockets. If the half-breed had received payment for the attempted murder, however, there was no trace of it.

He went back through the light-falling snow to Straw Topper and toed him onto his back, and was just about to search the fellow's pockets when a voice off to his right barked, 'Hold it right there, you thievin' sonofabitch!'

For a moment Cannon froze, still bent over. Then, slowly, he turned his head until he could see the speaker as he came out of the trees.

He was about fifty, but living out here had made him old before his time. He was short and thin, with a weathered, nut-brown face that was hidden behind a shaggy beard the colour of dirty snow. He wore a battered fur felt hat with a curled brim, a heavy plaid jacket, grey wool pants and black stovepipe boots, and in his hands he held an ancient Volcanic repeating pistol.

Cannon said carefully, 'Go easy there, mister. This isn't what it looks like.'

'The hell it ain't!' spat the other. 'I got me a claim back yonder aways, heard the shootin', figured to come see what was goin' on, an' here I find you, stealin' from the poor souls you've just murdered.'

'Murder, hell,' Cannon replied, taking a chance and straightening to his full height. 'Look a little closer and you'll see that these two already had their guns drawn and were fixing to — '

Dismissing that with an irritable shake of the head, the newcomer suddenly barked, 'Did Dawson Jack send you? Is that it? An' don't try lyin' to me! Joe Daniels might not be the sharpest knife in the box, but he can spot a liar at forty paces! You try lyin' to me and I'll clean your damn' clock for you good!'

Cannon said levelly, 'I don't know anyone named Dawson Jack. I only got into town yesterday noon.'

'But you've already accounted for two poor travellers, is that it?'

'Listen up, Daniels. These sorry sonsofbitches lured me out here so they could kill me and rob me. If I'd been a *cheechako*, they'd have managed it, too.'

'But they didn't.'

'No, they didn't, because I shot them before they could shoot me.'

'And then you decided to rob 'em.'

Still wound tight from the recent action, Cannon snapped, 'Look at 'em. Do they look as if they'd be worth robbing?'

'Well, why else would you be goin' through their pockets?'

'Because I had a notion that they might've been paid to kill me, and I was looking for proof.'

'Money?'

'*Blood*-money, yeah.'

'Did you find any?'

'No.'

Joe Daniels studied him for a long, thoughtful moment. 'What makes you worth killin', anyway?' he asked at length.

'Damned if I know. My name's Cannon. I came out here to find a man named Emmet Lawrence. The 'breed over there said the man had a claim out this way and offered to take me to him. It just occurred to me that Lawrence might not want to be found.'

'Whyfore you after this man?'

'You ask a lot of questions, Daniels.'

'An' I'm still waitin' on an answer to the last one.'

'Lawrence's wife hired me to find him, or what became of him, after he stopped writing to her.'

'You don't mean this feller no harm, then?'

'No.'

Daniels pursed his lips. His brown

eyes fell briefly to the sorry-looking dead men again. At last the muzzle of the Volcanic dropped a notch. 'Looks like we're in for another blow,' he murmured with a glance at the sky. 'Tell you what. Go round up them horses an' we'll ruminate on this back at my cabin.'

Cannon finally allowed himself to relax. 'What about these two?' he asked, gesturing to the dead men.

Daniels shrugged. 'If they're as bad as you say, haul 'em off the trail and leave 'em for the wolves. That's the way of things out here.'

★ ★ ★

They headed south and west through the timber until, about half a mile on, the trees thinned and they came to a sluggish stream that was still covered in places by thin sheet ice. On the far side of the stream sat a small dugout beside an equally rough-and-ready pole corral, above which had been fixed a patched tarpaulin for shelter.

Daniels led him across some rough-hewn stepping stones and they off-saddled the Tlingits' mounts before turning them out into the corral with a pinch of hay. The miner had been right: the wind picked up and the snow began to fall thicker and faster. Shoulders hunched, he led Cannon down into a slit-trench at the end of which stood a sturdy pine door. All that was visible of the dugout itself was about eighteen inches of wall and a gently pitched sod roof. Everything else was below ground.

Cannon followed his host into the dugout. It was a dreary, poky little place that stank of timber, tobacco, sweat and gun-grease. Still, it hadn't been designed for comfort, just as a refuge from the weather, somewhere for its occupant to spend the time when he wasn't digging or panning. There was a narrow cot, a homemade table, chair and a tea chest that doubled as a cabinet, and a pile of dirty laundry, saddlebags and other paraphernalia in the far corner.

Daniels got a lantern going and then poked some life into the wind-whipped fire in the tiny hearth. He filled a pot with coffee beans and snowmelt water and set it on to boil.

'Dawson City,' he muttered as Cannon sat at the table. 'I wouldn't give a spit for the place! Den of iniquity, Cannon, a latter-day Sodom. Hardly ever show my face there, if I can help it. Prefer to trade with the Tagish or Tlingit Indians for whatever I need. Anyways, I like the peace an' quiet out here. Well, that's to say I *did*, till you showed up.'

He poured the coffee, handed one scratched enamel mug to his guest and cradled the other 'twixt his palms. ''Course, the town weren't so bad before Dawson Jack took over.'

Cannon blew on his coffee. 'Who *is* Dawson Jack, anyway?'

Daniels looked as if he might spit rust. 'Ever hear of a feller named Soapy Smith?'

'Sure.'

Smith was a near-legendary bunko artist and crime boss who'd started his criminal career in Colorado. More recently Cannon had heard that he'd moved in on Skagway, put the local law on his payroll and then built up a small army of henchmen to help him take control of the town.

'Well,' said Daniels, 'Jack Bleeker's jus' like him, a two-bit con man greedy for power, 'cept that his stampin'-ground's right here in Dawson City.'

'Bleeker,' Cannon repeated. 'I heard some men complaining about him last night.'

'That don't surprise me. He's got Dawson all sewn up. No matter what it is that you want — supplies, a drink, a bed for the night or even a woman — he makes sure you get charged top dollar for the privilege.'

'Sure sounds like a man to hate.'

'He is. An' I hate the sonofabitch more'n most. See, Bleeker an' me, we used to be partners.'

Cannon paused, then said, 'He

conned you too, did he?'

'Uh-huh. Stole my gold right out from under me an' used it to buy up half the city!' He stared moodily into his coffee. 'That really soured me, Cannon. Took away whatever faith I still had in human nature.'

'What happened?'

'I met him on the trail comin' up from 'Frisco. He struck me as a decent sort, an' we hit it off from the get-go. I allus figured we trusted each other, so when he suggested we go into partnership, I didn't even hesitate. Jack was an educated man, an' I reckoned that might come in handy if we struck it rich.

'Anyways, we shook on it. Weren't no need for contracts or signatures as far as I was concerned. I reckoned my handshake was good enough, an' so was his. But I was wrong. When we reached Dawson he registered our claim, jus' like he said he would — but in his name only.

'By the time I caught onto it, it was

too late. Found out afterwards that he'd been working the same scam all over, dupin' other unfortunates like myself, men of poor learnin' who should've knowed better but didn't. No wonder he told me not to spread word of our partnership around — he was doin' the same thing to just about everyone else he could trick!

''Course, he was speculatin', but in such a way that didn't cost him a dime. A lot of the claims he registered never amounted to a hill o' horse-dung, but others . . . well, they paid off in spades an' gave him the wherewithal he needed to start takin' over Dawson, lot by lot. By the time us fellers he'd gypped tried to go after him, it was too late. He'd already surrounded himself with a bunch of hired guns.'

'Why didn't you go to the law?'

''Cause by then he'd bought the law, too.'

'Evers?'

'You know him?'

'We've met.'

Daniels shook his head. 'No, they's no help for the likes of me. But that's my bad luck. An' that's why I s'pose I was so ready to think the worst an' stick a gun in your face back there on the trail. I got me a decent little claim here now, but it's always at the back of my mind that Dawson Jack'll send his gunsels down to take this place away from me, too.'

The wind suddenly picked up, making the roof creak and the small fire dance and flicker. 'What about this feller you been askin' after, anyways?' asked Daniels. 'Just how in the world you reckon to find your needle in this particular haystack?'

'Good question,' Cannon replied. 'For a while there I thought I was going to meet the man himself. Instead I helped two men meet their maker.'

★ ★ ★

Jack Bleeker stood at the window of his small office on the first floor of the

Monte Carlo Saloon and surveyed Dawson's main street through cool blue eyes. It was a little before midday and despite the weather the street was bustling. As usual, however, Bleeker had nothing but contempt for its hungry-looking inhabitants. They'd turned their backs on everything they knew in order to get rich quick. Not that he had anything against that. A man had to have ambition. That's what kept the world turning.

No, it was *failure* he despised, and the men and women down there reeked of it. They'd come to make their fortunes and the majority had given up at the first hurdle. When it came down to it, they had no grit, no determination, no staying power.

Bleeker smiled fleetingly. He was a tall, spare-looking man with a long, pale, sober face and curly black sideburns that swooped low to join the moustache adorning his upper lip, and he considered himself to be in a whole different league to the townsfolk he so despised. He'd sensed opportunity here in Dawson and had grasped it with both hands . . . but opportunity, as he saw it, meant the chance to fleece a more or less captive audience of every last penny they had.

It had paid off, too: and handsomely, if his finely tailored clothes — a spotless black frock coat with silk lapels over a double-breasted brocade vest and diamond-studded cravat — were any indicator.

Naturally, he'd needed capital first. And that was the beauty of the whole deal. He'd used the suckers' own money to finance his empire. On the way up from Frisco he'd deliberately befriended ten or twelve would-be diggers and suggested they go into partnership. They could see he was educated, a man of some breeding, but he'd also made sure they considered him to be scrupulously honest, maybe even slightly naïve.

It had been so easy to dupe them. Most had been only too happy to throw in with him, to handle all the physical work while he dealt with all the paperwork. And that's where they'd come unstuck.

Most of them could neither read nor write, but by the time he'd finished buttering them up they'd have trusted him with their lives. To an extent, they had.

Of course, it was hit and miss. Most of the claims he'd filed on behalf of his so-called 'partners' hadn't panned out. But five of them had. And the success of those claims had provided him with the money to hire guns and throw those same 'partners' off their claims and send his own hired men in to work them for him.

After that things had moved fast, and almost before anyone knew it, Jack Bleeker was the King of Dawson City, and there wasn't a damn' thing anyone could do about it. They had to drink his overpriced whiskey, pay through the nose to eat at his restaurants or sleep in his hotels or buy provisions at his stores or sleep with his whores. And that was just how he wanted it.

A soft rapping at the door interrupted his musings, and moving across to his desk he called, 'Come.'

The door swung open and Bob Evers came inside and nodded a greeting. 'Mornin', Mr Bleeker.'

As he took off his snow-covered hat, Bleeker sensed the other man's discomfort and, toying idly with his prized possession — a wildly uneven, fist-sized chunk of gold ore that doubled as a paperweight — said, 'What's on your mind, Bob?'

Evers came to stand before the desk, his manner subservient but his eyes showing just how much he really hated to kowtow. 'There's trouble again,' he said.

Bleeker sighed. 'There's always trouble, Bob. Deal with it.'

'It might not be that easy this time,' Evers said uncomfortably. 'You're pushing this town too hard, Mr Bleeker. I'm getting complaints.'

'About . . . ?'

'The usual. How you water your whiskey. How your whores are riddled

with the pox. How you inflate the prices
of everythin' you bring in. How you,
uh, 'discourage' the competition an'
collect protection money from the rest.
These folks are rough-and-ready, and
you can shove 'em around, to a point.
But they'll only take it for so long.'

'Meaning?'

'You've got the clout to scare just
about any man, Mr Bleeker. But when
one man becomes a mob, they get a
mite more courage.'

Bleeker frowned. 'Is that the word
going around? That they're planning
some sort of rebellion?'

'More or less.'

'Then hire a few men, crack a few
heads, knock some of the vinegar out of
them.'

'You can only intimidate them for so
long, Mr Bleeker. Why not . . . '

He seemed to dry up.

'Yes?'

'Why not put your prices down, at
least for a while, till this unrest blows
over?'

It was good advice, but advice that was impossible to take. For what Evers didn't understand, what none of them understood, was that he was racing against the clock here. At the moment there were only a handful of Mounties in the Yukon to enforce law and order, which meant that he could more or less do whatever he liked and get away with it. But a year from now there'd be hundreds, and then everything would change. He had to make his money before that happened.

'I think you're a mite addled, Bob,' he said at last. 'The miners don't run things around here, *I* do. Now, you go do some more listening, find out who's behind all this talk, the ringleaders. And then deal with them.'

'You mean kill 'em?'

'No. That'll only turn them into martyrs. But feel free to break any two items you like on each of the men you suspect of being behind this. That should set an example to the rest of them.'

Evers hesitated. 'I'm not sure I can do that, Mr Bleeker.'

'You'll do as you're damn' well told!'

But Evers stood his ground. 'I can close my eyes to this, to *you*, but I can't do it indefinitely. Those people you're gyppin', maybe they deserve it an' maybe they don't. But they're my people as well, and they're looking to me to make sure they get a fair shake!'

Bleeker's eyes grew flat. 'Any time you get tired of taking my money, Bob, just say so. 'Fact, you'd be doing me a favour. I've been thinking for a while now that maybe you should make way for a younger man.'

'Oh, I'll go,' said Evers, suddenly finding his nerve again. 'And it'll please me to do so. But I reckon I'll collect a bonus before I go.'

Bleeker made a sort of incredulous chuffing noise. 'Bonus?'

'Well, call it hush money, then,' said Evers, and he added very deliberately, 'Mr *Lawrence*.'

Bleeker's face paled. All at once the only thing that could be heard was the sound of laughter and shouting from downstairs, mixed in with the tinkling of a reasonably well-played piano. At last he broke it with a whispered question. 'What did you just say?'

'Lawrence,' repeated Evers. 'That is your real name, isn't it?'

'I don't know what you're gabbing about,' snapped Bleeker. 'But I think you'd better get out of here — for good.'

Evers nodded and clapped his hat back on. 'Your game's up, Lawrence. I don't know who you really are or why you changed your name, but I can tell you this much. Someone came to town yesterday looking for you. Lookin' for *Lawrence*. I've a mind to tell him where he can find you.'

Recovering himself, Bleeker said with a sneer, 'And what made you think Lawrence was me?'

'He's carryin' a photograph,' said Evers. 'A real *good* one.' A twisted smile touched his lips. 'Tough-looking *hombre*, the man

156

lookin' for you. The kind who doesn't quit.'

Bleeker got up and went back to the window. Without looking around, he said, 'Got a name, this tough-looking *hombre* of yours?'

'Now that'd be telling,' said Evers. 'Just like it'd be telling was I to let him know where he could find you.'

Bleeker said, 'How much of a bonus are we talking about?'

Evers shrugged. 'I'm not a greedy man,' he said, adding pointedly, 'Unlike some. Let's say ten grand.'

'Let's say five,' said Bleeker. 'It's yours, provided you give me his name, where I can find him and then get the hell out of the territory.'

'Deal,' Evers said with a relieved grin. 'But I'll take the money first.'

'I thought you might.'

Bleeker went to the Jenks & Millbush safe in the corner, bent and fiddled with the wheel. Over one shoulder he said, 'The name?'

'Cannon. Tom Cannon.'

'What does he look like?'

'Big. Grey eyes, short fair hair. He says he's working for your wife.'

Again Bleeker froze for a moment. Then: 'Where can I find him?'

'The Miner's Rest.'

Bleeker nodded, opened the safe door and reached inside. A moment later he withdrew his hand.

It was filled with a Colt .45.

Evers' eyes went round when he saw it. 'Whoa, there! What the hell — ?'

Bleeker came upright and said, 'It'll be a cold day in hell before I give you anything save a bullet, Bob.'

Evers' fear was quickly replaced by fury. 'You haven't got the stomach for it,' he said, reaching for his own Colt.

But he was wrong.

Bleeker did have the stomach for it.

The street was so noisy and the saloon downstairs so busy that the single gunshot went unnoticed by all but one man, whose job it was to pay attention to such things. Within seconds, there came a hammering on the door. 'Mr Bleeker?

You all right in there?'

Recognizing the voice of Nelson Valliere, Bleeker said, 'Come in.' In the wake of the gunshot, his voice was high and strained. Ordering men to be killed came easy to him. Doing the job himself did not.

It did to Valliere. A tall, lean-flanked thirty year-old Creole of French and Spanish descent, he fairly burst into the room with a Cavalry Colt in his dark fist, pulling up sharp when he saw the body on the floor, and the blood leaking lazily from the deceptively small hole in its chest.

He took a closer look at the face, recognized Evers and said, 'Wha' happened?'

He was a swarthy man, dark-haired, with a long, baby-smooth face, high cheekbones and eyes the colour of copper pennies, dressed in a high-crowned slouch hat and a Worsted wool flannel suit, the jacket unbuttoned to reveal the fancy, wine-coloured vest beneath. The gun-belt around his hips looked at odds with the suit, but it was a crucial tool of

Valliere's trade. That and his heavy accent — a leftover from his tough childhood in Louisiana — were his most memorable features.

Bleeker put the gun back into the safe, shut the door, spun the wheel, then he went to the side cabinet and poured himself a whiskey.

'Evers got ideas above his station,' he replied at last. 'I was forced to, uh, let him go.'

Valliere nodded. Like Bleeker, he'd come north in search of riches, but he'd figured to make money from his single greatest talent, his ability with a gun. Bleeker had been the highest bidder for his services, and now Valliere was perhaps the closest of all Bleeker's associates, though even he didn't know the whole truth.

'I get rid of him,' he said practically. 'Get the blood off the carpet, too, before it stain.'

Bleeker's whiskey disappeared in one swallow. 'I've got another job for you, Nels.'

Valliere eyed him expectantly.

'There's a man staying at the Miner's Rest, a man name of Tom Cannon. Take a couple of men and make sure he doesn't see tomorrow's sunrise.'

Valliere nodded. He was not by nature a curious man. It never troubled him to know the why of things. A job was a job. He did it and got paid for it, and that was all that mattered to him.

'Oh, and Nels?'

'Yeah?'

'This man. By all accounts, he's carrying a photograph of me. I want it.'

The Creole nodded. 'Consider it done.'

'And watch yourself,' Bleeker added, stopping him with his hand on the doorknob. 'I'm led to believe that this man Cannon knows how to handle himself.'

Valliere's teeth showed fiercely white in his coffee-coloured face. 'Good,' he said. 'I like a challenge.'

Left alone but for the corpse, Bleeker allowed himself a shudder and flopped into his chair. An image of Lorna crept into his head, and he thought with near-childish petulance, *Why can't you leave me alone?*

At first he'd considered himself lucky to have won her heart. But her family had never accepted him, for he had not come from their world. All they had ever known was money and privilege. He was from a lower class, a sorry sonofabitch whose love had been genuine, but whose motives had always been suspect. Lorna had loved him, but her parents had despised him for the scheming, money-grabbing low-life they believed him to be.

So he had taken it into his head to make his own fortune, and prove them wrong. And once the idea took root it became almost an obsession: to make more money than they had ever hoped to have, and turn the tables so that he could look down his nose at *them*.

But then Lorna had changed. Perhaps, because of the obvious disdain with which her parents had always treated him, she had become over-protective. But it was probably closer to the truth to say that her true character — her possessive nature, her constant jealously, the need in her to control him from dawn till dusk, day in, day out — had become ever more apparent.

Whatever the case, when he set sail for the Yukon, he quickly discovered that he was glad to be free of her: relieved, almost. Away from Lorna he finally became the man he really was and had always aspired to be, a man who had power, position and wealth, a man who could command and receive respect and fear in equal measure, who could dictate who should live and who should die.

But this man Cannon, whom Lorna had dispatched to find him . . . it made him feel uneasy. It reminded him that he hadn't escaped from Lorna's clutches after all. But get rid of Cannon and maybe Lorna would think twice before sending anyone else on such a fool's errand.

His thoughts turned to Valliere. The man had many good points. He was cool, efficient and loyal — as long as the money kept rolling in. But there was also a dark, sadistic side to him. He enjoyed his work perhaps a little too much.

He went back to the cabinet and poured himself another whiskey, being careful not to look at the body cooling on the floor. *I must be getting soft*, he thought. *I almost feel sorry for this man Cannon.*

9

It was a little after four in the afternoon when Cannon got back to town, and the mixture of heavy cloud and twilight had already darkened the sky considerably. He returned Natuk's horse to the livery stable and, deliberately keeping it as vague as possible, explained that his own mount had sustained an injury in the bad weather and had to be put down. To make amends he offered up Straw Topper's horse as a replacement, and after giving the creature a thorough inspection, the liveryman pronounced himself satisfied with the exchange and said no more about it. It was, as Joe Daniels had told him, the way of things in the Yukon.

The snow had finally stopped and the wind had calmed at last, and as he walked back to the Miner's Rest he considered his next move. It had been a long, fruitless day and his priority right now was to thaw out and then go get something to eat. After that he'd start over again, this time showing his picture of Lawrence around in Dawson's many saloons in the hope that someone somewhere would recognize the man.

The foyer was empty when he reached the hotel, so he helped himself to his key and then went upstairs. He knew that he should call in on Moore and Tyson first, just to let them know what had happened, but there'd be time enough for that over a meal and a drink later on. Instead he unlocked the door and let himself into his darkened room.

Too late he realized he wasn't alone.

He heard the tell-tale whisper of cloth against cloth an instant before his assailant punched him hard in the kidneys, and as his legs went out from under him he lost his grip on the shotgun. He took another punch in the back and then, suddenly, there were two of them, and as they crowded him the second one kneed him in the face and he fell back against the wardrobe, bleeding from the nose.

He made a grab for his Colt, but the sound of another weapon being brought to full cock, coupled with the feel of its cold, hard muzzle being rammed into the soft flesh behind his right ear, froze him in his tracks.

For a second the room was filled with hard, heavy breathing. Then there came the scratch and flare of a match, and dull amber light chased the shadows up across the ceiling.

The third man, the one holding the match, lit the lamp on the bedside table and turned it up high. Butter-coloured light filled the room.

Clenching his teeth against the pain in his lower back, Cannon looked from one of his attackers to the other. The man who'd almost busted his nose was short and wide, about forty, with the flushed, worn face of a heavy drinker. His companion, the one who'd punched him in the kidneys and now had him covered with the gun, was younger by at least a decade. He was gangly-tall, with dark features and a heavy jaw.

The man who'd lit the lantern looked down at him through eyes like copper pennies. He was tall and slim, dressed in a grey suit, and he wore a Cavalry Colt in the holster tied to his right thigh. His dark skin spoke of Latin blood. He was, Cannon thought, a Creole.

'You got a picture,' said Nelson Valliere. 'I want it.'

Cannon frowned, trying to make sense of the request. 'Did Evers send you?'

Ignoring him, Valliere said again, 'The photograph.'

'I heard you the first time,' Cannon bit back, slowly, carefully rising to one knee. 'But if Evers sent you, or maybe even Lawrence himself — '

At a gesture from Valliere, the man on his right, the gangly man with the overlarge jaw, started to make a vicious swiping movement with his gun, figuring to knock a few of Cannon's teeth loose.

Instead, Cannon powered up off the floor, grabbed his arm by wrist and elbow and broke it with a short, sharp crack.

As the man squealed and the gun dropped from his nerveless fingers, Cannon dodged behind him so that he became a human shield, and at the same time hooked his own gun from its Hardin shoulder-rig and shoved it against the sobbing man's temple.

'Back off,' he barked. 'Shuck your guns and get your hands up!'

Valliere only smiled, but the part-time drunk to Cannon's left played it differently. With an elaborate show of defeat, and using only his thumb and forefinger, he slowly started to lift his .41-calibre Colt Model 1889 from its pocket, but he didn't fool Cannon for a moment.

At the last second he snatched the Colt out and up, but Cannon's gun blasted first and the part-time drunk's yell turned to a scream as Cannon's bullet hammered him in the right shoulder and he fell backwards, into the bedside table. The table rocked and the lamp tipped over and smashed against the carpet. Kerosene splashed everywhere and ignited at once.

The Creole finally made his move. His gun came up in a silver arc, but Cannon shoved his human shield towards him just as he fired his shot. The bullet punched into the gangly man, suddenly checking his forward momentum. Cannon raised his Colt, drew a bead on Valliere but at the last moment caught a flicker of movement off to his left and realized that the part-time drunk had snatched his gun back up, left-handed this time.

He twisted and fired again: his bullet hit the man in the chest high and centre and sent him spilling backwards, into and through the window.

The glass shattered with a loud rattle and the part-time drunk vanished into the darkness. Above the roar of the spreading flames Cannon heard the bone-breaking thud he made landing in the snow-packed yard below.

He dropped to a crouch just as Valliere fired again. The bullet chunked into the wardrobe door. He raised the gun to return fire but suddenly Valliere was no longer there. He heard the man's boots pounding against the floorboards outside and considered giving chase, but by now the hotel's other occupants had been drawn by the sound of gunfire and he heard men yelling, and at least one woman demanding to know what in hell was going on. It was possible that they could get caught in the crossfire if he went after the Creole.

In any case, the carpet was ablaze now, and it needed putting out before the fire spread. He tore a blanket off the bed and started to beat at it. When he heard a sound behind him a few seconds later he spun so fast that Henson Moore flinched.

'I surrender!' the old man said, coughing, then stepped over the gangly man's body, grabbed a second blanket and started beating at the flames with his good arm. 'What the hell happened here?'

'Someone somewhere doesn't want me to find Lawrence,' Cannon replied, sniffing up blood. 'Question is, *who?*'

'Might be able to answer that shortly,' Moore said mysteriously.

'Huh?'

'That feller who took off like his pants was afire? Button lit out after him, to see where he'd go.'

Cannon didn't know whether to be mad or grateful. If Tyson could find out where the Creole went, it would certainly simplify matters for him. But if the Creole should suspect that he was being followed . . .

Just then the hotel owner stormed in behind a solid-looking deputy, who looked from the man on the floor to the shattered window and then said, 'What the hell's been going on here, feller?'

By now the fire was out, but the smoke-filled room stank of charred wood and burnt dust. Swiping the last of the blood from his nose, Cannon said, 'Three men were waiting for me when I came in. They were after robbing me, but I didn't give them the chance.'

'So I see,' growled the deputy. 'Can you prove it?'

'I'm his witness,' Moore offered swiftly. 'I was in the next room an' I heard the whole thing. 'You got the look of a rich man,' they says. 'Give us your loot.' Then there was a scuffle, an' some gunshots.'

The deputy considered that. He had a long nose and teeth that were so white and even that they just had to be store-bought. 'I see one body,' he said. 'Mr Barnswell here says there's a second litterin' up his backyard. Where's the third?'

'Lit out.'

'What's he look like?'

'Tall, thin, dark hat.'

'Well, someone's gonna have to pay for the damage,' said the indignant hotel owner, Barnswell.

'Them,' said Cannon, gesturing to

the body on the floor.

The deputy nodded. 'Sounds fair, in the circumstances. All right, Barnswell, send your hired boy for the undertaker. As for you, mister, better stick around a while. I might have some more questions for you.'

'Sure.' Cannon tossed his fire-blackened blanket onto the bed. 'By the way, deputy, where can I find Evers this time of day?'

'Mister,' said the deputy, halfway out the door, 'I wish I knew. Ain't seen hide nor hair of him since this morning.'

Left alone again, Moore shivered as an icy blast came in through the broken window. 'Better share with us tonight, Tom,' he muttered.

Cannon nodded, gathered up his gear and followed the old man next door, still thinking about the Creole and why he was so interested in the photograph of Lawrence. Evers was the only man he'd shown the picture to. Had he known more than he'd let on?

In Moore's room he washed up and

helped himself to a shot of the old man's whiskey to dull the pain in his kidneys. About twenty minutes later they heard footsteps outside and exchanged a look, for Moore had been as concerned for Tyson's welfare as Cannon was. A moment later Tyson let himself inside, his thin face flushed with excitement.

'I did good, Mr Cannon,' he reported eagerly. 'Found out where that bush-whacker went to, an' got his name while I was about it.'

'He didn't see you following him?'

'No sir. I tailed him to a saloon called the Monte Carlo. It's about three blocks east. He went inside an' upstairs an' I didn't see him again, so I asked one of the bartenders who he was and they told me his name was Nelson Va . . . Vall-i-ere, an' that he worked for a man named Dawson Jack Bleeker.'

Cannon frowned. There was that name again. It seemed to be haunting him. Reaching for his hat he said, 'Thanks, Jeff. You did better than good.'

Watching him head for the door, Tyson frowned. 'Where you goin'?'

'To have a few words with Valliere.'

Moore jumped up. 'Well, I reckon we'll go along with ye,' he said.

'No you won't, Henson. You two have done enough.'

Moore pulled a face. 'Confound you, Tom . . . '

But he was too late.

Cannon had already closed the door softly behind him.

★ ★ ★

He couldn't have missed the Monte Carlo if he'd tried. It stood two storeys high and took up almost half the block. He paused for a moment on the opposite boardwalk, listening to the sounds of revelry coming from within. The hitch-racks out front were full, as was the stable out back. Despite the high prices, business was obviously good.

At last he crossed the street, still

feeling stiff and sore-headed from his earlier run-in with Valliere's men but determined to satisfy that old curiosity of his with a few answers.

He pushed through the frosted-glass swing doors and went inside. The large main room was ablaze with the light from two fancy wagon-wheel chandeliers, and the alcohol-sweet air was warmed by three pot-bellied stoves. A long oak and brass bar ran the length of the facing wall, behind which a small army of smartly-attired bartenders busily dispensed cheer. Men of all types were either bellied up to the bar, conversing in groups or playing cards at scattered baize-topped tables, far more than he could count.

Saloon girls in crimson silk weaved between them, delivering drinks, sharing jokes and urging the customers to spend their money. Three shotgun-toting bouncers watched everything from strategically-placed high chairs.

Down at the far end of the room, a wide, carpeted staircase led up to a gallery and the rooms and offices above. In the nook beneath the gallery a pianist was playing something flowery and sentimental.

Cannon scanned the room until his eyes finally snagged on the man he was after. The Creole was leaning against the far end of the bar, not far from the piano, and splashing whiskey into a shot glass. Cannon weaved through the patrons with a slow, definite stride, not once daring to take his eyes off the man he'd come to question and just maybe kill.

Some sixth sense in Valliere, a survival instinct borne of long years as a hired gun, suddenly made him look up. When he saw Cannon moving toward him he pushed away from the bar and hung his right hand above the grips of his Colt, but to his surprise Cannon's only response was a grave-yard smile.

Coming to a halt barely four feet away, he said, 'You left before we'd properly finished our, ah, discussion.'

Valliere gave a cautious shrug. 'I di'n't

think there was anything lef' to say.'

'You mentioned a photograph. What photograph might that be?'

'You tellin' me you don't know?'

'Look, we're both busy men,' Cannon said tiredly. 'Suppose we just get down to cases. What's your interest in the photograph?'

'I got no interest.'

'Then who has?'

Valliere's grin was insolent, deliberately calculated to anger his opponent and force him into doing something rash. 'Beats me.'

Cannon pursed his lips. 'Aw, I'm sorry you said that,' he replied. 'Because I can see now that we're going to have to do this the hard way.'

He clenched his fists, waiting for Valliere to make his play. When he did, he'd planned to crowd the man before his gun could clear leather and then use the whiskey bottle to put him down for a while.

But all at once he sensed a presence behind him, and a low, cultured voice said, 'Don't be so hasty, Mr Cannon. I'm the man you're looking for.'

Skin tingling, he turned slowly until he came face to face with the man whose image he had only previously seen on hard photographic card.

'Lawrence,' he said softly.

'Bleeker,' corrected the other.

Over Cannon's shoulder, Valliere raised his eyebrows. He wanted to know if he should take Cannon while his back was turned. Bleeker gave his head the smallest shake. He didn't want any gunplay here. It would be bad for business, if only in the short term.

'Why don't we discuss the matter in my office?' he suggested. 'I'm sure it will be to our mutual advantage.'

Cannon hesitated briefly, then said, 'All right. Lead on.'

Lawrence — *Bleeker* — turned and glided back through the crowd. No one around them, save maybe the bouncers, seemed aware of just how close it had come to violence. Cannon followed him and Valliere fetched up the rear. They went up the staircase to the gallery above, then along a narrow corridor to a door at the far end. Bleeker opened the door and gestured for Cannon to go in ahead of him. As he did so, Bleeker told Valliere to wait outside.

Bleeker came into the office and closed the door behind him. Almost at once the sounds of music and laughter downstairs quietened to a distant murmur. Bleeker went around to his desk and sat down, then gestured that Cannon should take the visitor's chair.

'How's Lorna?' he asked after a moment.

'Worried sick about you.'

'Really?'

'Why else would she have sent me to find out what had become of you?'

Bleeker grimaced. 'Because she has a possessive streak a mile wide, Mr Cannon. Because she had me right where she wanted me, under her thumb, and because I escaped, which doesn't set well with her at all.'

'That's not the way I saw it.'

'Well, that's the way it was. But no

matter. You came to find out what had become of Emmet Lawrence. All right: go back and tell Lorna that he died. After all, it's no lie. Somewhere between Frisco and here, Emmet Lawrence did die. And Jack Bleeker was born.'

'I can't do that, Lawrence. Your wife paid me to get the truth, and that's what I aim to deliver.'

'Then how much do you want to deliver *my* version of the truth?'

'I wouldn't take a single red cent from you. From everything I've heard, I don't think I'd care too much for how you got it.'

'So where does that leave us?'

'It doesn't leave 'us' anywhere,' Cannon said, rising. 'I was hired to find out what had become of you. Now that I know, I can go back to Frisco and give your wife the straight of it. That you ran out on her.'

'But that's *not* the straight of it!' snapped Bleeker. 'I didn't plan to run out on anyone! I didn't even realize how stifling Lorna really was until I got away from her! It was only then that I promised myself that I'd never go back. I had dreams, an empire to build, money to make. I could never have done that as Lorna's husband!'

'That's not my concern.'

'Maybe not. But tell Lorna what I've done here and her family will tell her that they were right about me all along, and that's not true!'

Cannon smiled briefly. 'So you've still got some pride?'

'Pride, vanity, call it what you will. Besides, you don't know Lorna. Tell her I'm dead and she'll have to let the matter go. But tell her I'm still alive and she'll never rest until she gets me back.'

'I think you flatter yourself.'

'Oh, I'm not talking about love. I'm talking about jealousy! No one has ever walked out on her family before, and she'll move heaven and earth to make sure I'm not the first. She'll send others just like you.'

'Well, maybe you can buy the next one off.'

'Oh, no. I don't plan on spending the rest of my days looking over my shoulder, Cannon. This ends *here*.'

Cannon sighed. 'I'm going now, Lawrence, and I'll be pulling out in the morning. Don't try and stop me, because after I've finished with your pet gunman, I'll come for you . . . and you won't like that one bit.'

Bleeker's eyes dropped from his. 'If that's your last word on the subject,' he murmured.

'It is.'

Cannon turned and headed for the door, his thoughts turning now to Valliere, waiting outside. Had he heard the conversation? Would he greet Cannon with a drawn gun?

He neither saw nor heard Bleeker snatch up the fist-sized gold ore paperweight and come around the desk after him until it was too late.

Dawson Jack rushed at him, a weird, strangled cry falling from his lips as he screwed up the courage to do what he'd set out to do. He brought the paperweight down hard on Cannon's nape and Cannon, caught by surprise, crashed forward into the door. Bleeker hit him again: blood stained the edge of the paperweight: and then Cannon went down and didn't move again.

Hearing the sound he made falling, Valliere shouldered through the door with gun in hand. He almost tripped on the body.

'Is he . . .' croaked Bleeker, dropping the paperweight. 'Did I kill him?'

Valliere knelt, felt for a pulse at Cannon's throat and found one. 'Not yet.' He grinned. 'Wan' to hit him some more?'

Bleeker glared at him. 'Get him out of here,' he said. 'Take him someplace quiet and finish him off and then bury him.'

Valliere smiled. 'It'll be a pleasure.'

10

For a long, long time there nothing
but darkness and silence. Then Cannon
realized that someone was slapping him
roughly and telling him to wake the hell
up.

He tried to fight against regaining
consciousness. He was happier right
where he was. But then the pain hit him
hard in the head, a skull-ache like he'd
never known, and before he could do
anything about it he had to roll onto his
side and throw up.

'At last,' said a voice above him.

Cannon reluctantly opened his
eyes. At first everything was misty and
out of focus. Then he became aware of
the cold wind on his skin, of his skin
tightening against it, and he realized
that he was outdoors somewhere,
stretched out in thick snow: that he was
in some kind of clearing surrounded by

bare-branch trees and that he could see the purple night sky beyond them, the underbellies of the scudding clouds painted a strange powder-blue.

Finally Nelson Valliere stepped into view.

Sight of the man brought everything back in a heady rush. Bleeker had hit him, knocked him cold. And while he was unconscious they must've fetched him from the Monte Carlo to this lonely spot.

Blearily he looked around. Beyond Valliere stood a Murphy wagon hitched to a two-horse team: the wagon they'd doubtless used to bring him out here. And beside the wagon stood another man, smoking a quirley and stamping his feet against the cold.

Without warning pain exploded in Cannon's side, and he rolled the opposite way, curled up and grunted through clamped teeth. The same pain came again, and then once more, and he realized that Valliere was kicking him.

'I am a man of few rules,' the Creole muttered, watching him hunch up. 'But there is one abou' which I am mos' particular. I deman' respect. And anyone who do'n' show it . . . well, they have to be taught. No' for their own benefit. The men I teach don' usually live long enough for that. But as a lesson to *others*.'

On hands and knees now, Cannon tucked up under the repeated blows, and though his thinking was slowed by pain and cold, he knew he had to find a way to fight back. If he didn't, he was finished for sure.

Valliere kicked him again, and his hands folded hard into the snow.

'You' learning you' lesson now, huh?' said Valliere.

Cannon nodded slowly.

Then he twisted and threw a fistful of snow straight into Valliere's face.

Caught unawares, the Creole lurched backwards, and Cannon pushed up and leapt at him, not wanting to, not especially able to, but knowing he had to. He swung a clumsy roundhouse right that missed and suddenly the world started spinning again and he stumbled back to his knees.

'*Fils de pute!*' hissed Valliere, drawing his foot back for another kick.

At the same moment the sudden thunder of a shotgun blast stopped everything in its tracks, and as the shell tore through the wagon's canvas awning, a voice called, 'Reach fer the clouds, fellers, an' make it quick! We're a mite short on patience tonight!'

Instinctively the man by the wagon threw his quirley down and grabbed for the gun at his hip, but a second blast ripped through the night and a .10-gauge shell slammed him backwards against the sideboards, bleeding from the chest. He went down with barely a murmur.

Valliere heeled toward the sound of the shot, his Colt appearing to leap into his hand, but even as he peppered the darkness with return fire he sensed more than heard a sound behind him and spun back again. He saw a man

— an old man — scurrying across the clearing with a stout branch held club-like in his one good hand and quickly worked the hammer again —

A second later Henson Moore brought the makeshift weapon around in a wide arc and smashed the Creole right off his feet. Valliere flew sideways, struck the snow, squirmed for a few seconds, then lay still.

'Tom?' called Moore, as he threw down the branch and hurried over to his friend. 'You all right, son?'

Tyson trotted out of the darkness, holding Cannon's still-smoking shotgun. He looked pale and scared, and made a point of not looking at the man he'd just shot dead. 'Is he all right?' he asked nervously.

'Unconscious,' said Moore, still breathing hard from his exertions. He looked around. 'Let's get him into yonder wagon, button. We don't patch him up pronto, we'll lose him for sure.'

Cannon regained a hazy kind of consciousness as they lifted him into the back of the wagon. 'H-Henson?' he croaked. 'That you?'

'It's me, Tom.'

'Wha . . . what the hell are you . . . doing here?'

'Me 'n' Jeff, we didn't much cotton to bein' left behind at the hotel, so we come after you, an' a good thing for you that we did. We was just in time to see them sons carryin' you down the alley beside the Monte Carlo an' dumpin' you in a wagon at the livery stable. We'd've been here sooner, but we had to go rent hosses so's we could give chase.'

'I'm . . . obliged.'

'Good. Now set quiet. We're takin' you back to town.'

'B-better not, Greybeard. Bleeker'll . . . turn that place upside down once he finds out I'm still around.'

Moore considered. 'Well, we can't leave you out here. 'Sides, you need patchin' up, boy. You look like hell.'

As much as he wanted to sleep his assorted hurts away right then, Cannon forced himself to think for a moment, then said, 'I . . . think I know a place I can . . . hole up. You just . . . go where I tell you.'

Moore and Tyson traded glances. Then Moore said, 'Go fetch the horses, button, an' tie 'em to the tailgate. I guess we better do like the man says.'

★ ★ ★

Joe Daniels was asleep in his dugout when the wagon rattled into his yard. As Tyson hauled on the reins, Moore raised his voice above the wind and called, 'You in there, Joe Daniels?'

A few seconds later an oblong shutter in the side of the dugout was drawn back and the business end of the miner's ancient Volcanic pistol showed itself. 'I'm here, an' I'm armed! Who are you?'

'Friends of Tom Cannon,' said Moore. 'He's been hurt, Daniels, an' we're hopin' you might let him fort up here till he gets better.'

There came no immediate response. Then: 'What's happened to him?'

'Jack Bleeker damn'-near bashed his brains out, an' his pet gunman came close to finishin' the job for him, till we showed up.'

'An' who're you?'

'My name's Moore. The button beside me's called Tyson. Now, you gonna help us with Tom, or you gonna turn us away?'

Again Daniels was silent for a long moment, while he considered what he'd been told. Then the gun disappeared and the miner said, 'I'll help. But this better not be a trick.'

A moment later he came outside, his gun in one hand, a lantern held high in the other. He moved around to the back of the wagon and peered inside. One look at Cannon's battered face confirmed Moore's story.

'Let's get him inside,' he said. 'Then you fellers can tell me what this is all about.'

It was a long night, but Cannon didn't know much about it. Once they'd transferred him to Daniels' narrow cot, Moore examined him carefully and concluded that he had concussion and cracked ribs. There was nothing they could do for the former save keep an eye on him when he finally regained consciousness, but to help with the latter they bandaged his ribs as tight as they dared.

At last, over coffee, Moore told Daniels as much as they knew.

'Well, Cannon's welcome to stay here as long as it takes,' Daniels said when he'd finished. 'But I don't care much for his colour. Be lucky if he makes it through till dawn.'

'He'll make it,' said Moore. 'He's too tough to die, 'specially when he's still got unfinished business needs tendin'.'

Around dawn he and Tyson left their friend in Daniels' care. 'We're stayin' at the Miner's Rest, iffen you need to reach us,' said Moore.

'Don't fret,' replied Daniels. 'I'll look after him. When he comes round he's gonna have a powerful hate for Bleeker. I'm kinda curious to see what he does about it.'

★ ★ ★

Daniels was a good host, and when Moore and Tyson rode back out to the dugout four days later, they found Cannon pale but well enough to be up and around . . . and to give the stocky, mostly silent man they'd fetched with them a wary scrutiny.

'How you feelin', Mr Cannon?' asked Tyson.

'Still drawing breath, thanks to you fellers.'

'Shucks,' said Moore. 'T'weren't nothin'.' Then he glanced at the man beside them and sobered. 'Tom, this here's Ezra Teal. He's been speakin' out on behalf of the miners, tryin' to get Bleeker to give 'em a fairer deal.'

'I saw you outside Bob Evers' office the night we first got into town,' said Cannon, shaking with him.

'Well, they's been a few, ah, 'developments' since then,' said Moore.

As they settled themselves, he continued, 'You were right about Bleeker. His men've just about turned Dawson inside out, lookin' for you. An' that Creole feller, Valliere, he's just as mad.'

'He's still alive, then?'

'Let's jus' say his skull must'a been tougher than I thought.'

Teal chose that moment to speak. He had broad shoulders and a square face, most of which was obscured by a dusty black beard. 'They tell me you got a score to settle with Bleeker, Mr Cannon,' he said evenly. 'Well, so have we. Bleeker's pushed us just about as far as we're willin' to go. Final straw came yest'day. A miner named Proctor refused to pay Bleeker's men protection money. He turned up dead yest'day mornin', shot in the back. It's clear the law won't do anythin' about it, so I guess it's up to us.'

'Trouble is,' Moore went on, 'Bleeker's heard all the fightin' talk around town, an' he's not takin' any chances. He's surrounded himself with a small army, Tom. No one can get to him till they've got through them.'

Cannon fell silent for a while. Then he said, 'What's your plan, Ezra?'

'Haven't got one,' Teal replied honestly. 'We jus' figure to storm the Monte Carlo, drag Bleeker out of there and string the bastard up.'

'You'll get a lot of men killed that way. Men who don't deserve it.'

'You got a better idea?'

Cannon said, 'I think I have. How many men can you rely on?'

'Thirty, at least. Good men, Mr Cannon, not apt to crack or let us down.'

'You can add me to that list,' growled Daniels.

'All right,' said Cannon. 'This is how we're going to do it . . . '

A bitter wind blew through Dawson two nights later, carrying with it the first stray flakes of a new blizzard, and for once the town seemed curiously muted.

Cannon stood in an alley opposite the Monte Carlo, trying to ignore his aching ribs. Although he was mending by the day, the ride in from Daniels' dugout had close to killed him. Now he checked his pocket watch. It was a little after nine-thirty. If Bleeker or Valliere had been expecting trouble, it would have happened long before this. With any luck they'd be letting their guard drop about now. They'd made it through another day.

He heard footsteps behind him and he and Daniels turned as Moore and Tyson hustled out of the darkness to join them. 'You made it, then,' said Moore.

'Did you think we'd miss it?' countered Daniels.

Moore studied Cannon concernedly. 'You sure you're up to this?'

'Quit fretting, Henson. I'm fine.'

'Here,' said Tyson, handing Cannon his shotgun.

Cannon took it and quickly checked it over. It was loaded with five ten-gauge shot-shells, and he had a feeling that he'd need every one before this night was over.

'You two don't have to take a hand in this,' he said at last.

'That's what I've been tellin' the button, here,' muttered Moore. 'But he's as set on it as I am.'

'He's right, Mr Cannon,' added Tyson, nerves making him look far younger than his seventeen years. 'Sometimes a man has to stand up and do what's right.'

Daniels clapped him on the shoulder. 'Can't argue with that.'

'Are you both armed?' asked Cannon.

Moore nodded. 'Ayuh. Ezra Teal rustled us up a sixgun each.'

'Well, if it comes to shooting, keep

your heads down, the three of you. I haven't got so many friends that I can afford to lose any. Got that?'

'Got it.'

Cannon tightened his jaw and worked the lever to put a shell under the hammer. 'All right,' he said. 'Let's do it.'

They crossed the street shoulder to shoulder and went up onto the far boardwalk. How things went over the next few minutes hinged on the miners, on whether or not they'd been able to spot and mark their targets ahead of time, and how well they could hold their nerve once they'd done it. If they did as they were told, they might all come through this in one piece. If not, it was going to be a bloodbath.

Cannon pushed inside with Moore, Tyson and Daniels following him.

The saloon was doing good business, but it was nowhere near as busy as it had been the last time Cannon was there. The word had obviously gone out that tonight would be a bad night to visit the Monte Carlo. That alone might tip Bleeker and Valliere that something was in the wind. But Cannon had told his makeshift army to warn their friends off. If it did come to shooting, he wanted to keep the casualties to a minimum.

He paused a moment inside the doorway and scanned the place, seeing at once that Bleeker had indeed surrounded himself with a small army. Scattered throughout the saloon, at the bar, at tables, or just standing hipshot in corners, were hard-faced men with busy eyes: more than a dozen who made the causing and settling of trouble their business. Add those to the three bouncers sitting in their high chairs with their shotguns across their laps and you had a formidable army indeed.

Valliere was across the room, leaning against the counter nursing a whiskey. The left side of his face still showed signs of bruising and swelling, where Moore had smashed him off his feet with the tree-branch. He spotted

Cannon the minute he came inside: Cannon saw his shoulders stiffen, watched him step away from the counter, saw him smile, actually smile, and flex the fingers of his gun-hand expectantly.

Mouth tight, Cannon began to stride between tables, heading for him, and as he went, so he brought silence with him, as drinkers glanced around and saw the promise of trouble in his flat stare, in the way he held the shotgun across his chest, the bullet-straight line he made for Valliere.

Bleeker's hired guns saw it too, and started reaching for iron.

This is it, Cannon thought. *If Teal's men let me down now, it's all over.*

But Teal's men didn't let him down. Earlier that evening they'd drifted into the Monte Carlo in twos and threes, bought drinks they barely touched and then started looking for the men Cannon had told them to watch out for — Dawson Jack's hired guns.

Now, as those same hardcases started

to draw their weapons, the miners screwed up their nerve, drew their own weapons — a motley collection of ancient pocket pistols, double-action Remingtons, open-top Army revolvers and even a .32-calibre seven-shooter — and stuck them into spines or napes of necks or simply stepped between them and their target, and if they spoke at all it was to say, *Nope*, or *Better not*, or *I'd keep that smoke-wheel leathered, was I you.*

Moore glanced around and almost cackled with approval. 'Only quarrel we got here is with Bleeker an' this man Valliere!' he cried. 'Rest o' you folks want to avoid trouble, best you leave now!'

For a moment there was neither word nor movement. But few patrons needed telling twice, and they quickly scrambled to their feet and made for the doors, Bleeker's alarmed percentage girls among them.

The tension now was palpable, as the miners finally backed away from their marks and joined ranks with Ezra Teal on one side of the saloon, while Bleeker's hired gunnies and bouncers set themselves for a fight on the other.

Valliere's smile turned to a sneer. 'What the hell you think you're doing here, Cannon?'

'In the old days,' said Cannon, finally drawing to a halt, 'we called it running a man out on a rail.'

Valliere cocked an eyebrow. 'Bleeker?'

'All of you. These people have had enough, and I can't say that I blame 'em.' He glanced up at the gallery and called, '*Lawrence!* You hear that? It's over! The men with me are all for stringing you up, but they're willing to let you go free, provided you don't make trouble and you don't come back!'

There was no response from above, no sound, no movement.

'A lot of men stand to die if you decide to make a fight of it!'

Still nothing.

Cannon looked at Valliere. 'Looks like I'm going to have to go up and get him, then.'

Valliere slowly crossed to the stair-case, planted himself at the foot of the stairs and then flipped back the fold of his jacket to the reveal the grips of his long-barrelled Colt. 'You' have to get pas' me first,' he said.

'I figured that.'

'Then what you waitin' for?'

A gun-blast filled the room then, and Cannon threw himself sideways, rolled and came up behind a table just as splinters burst up from the boards where he'd just been standing. Snapping his head up, he saw Bleeker half-hidden behind one of the crimson drapes at the far end of the gallery, smoke wisping from his .45.

Another gunshot tore through the air, and Cannon switched his gaze to Valliere, who'd drawn his own gun and was fixing to nail him while the nailing was good. Cannon flinched, swore, told himself that he might have known they wouldn't settle this thing peacefully, then came around the table, not over it, snap-aimed and fired the shotgun.

The shell ripped into Valliere's chest and threw him backwards across the first few steps of the staircase, and the kick of the shotgun sent a wave of agony through Cannon's cracked ribs.

Valliere was finished, but around him all hell was breaking loose, for Bleeker had given his men just the distraction they needed to make their move.

At once the big room was filled with gunfire, and men scurrying for cover. As Cannon shoved the table over he saw one of the bouncers stand tall on his high seat and draw a bead on Tyson. He pumped the Winchester and fired again, and the shell struck the bouncer dead centre of his bed-of-flowers vest and he flew sideways off the high chair and smashed a table to matchwood on his way to the floor.

A bullet whined close overhead. Another slapped into the tabletop. Cannon worked the action again, came around the table and yelled, 'Give it up!'

The gunman who'd been sighting on Ezra Teal heard his voice and twisted.

Flame spat from his Remington, but the shot was hasty and missed. Cannon fired back, blew a chunk from his right shoulder and sent him sprawling.

Another bullet slammed into the table, this time from someplace behind him. He fell sideways and rolled, again spotted Bleeker at the top of the stairs and fired again. The shotgun boomed and splintered baluster rails, but did no greater damage than that. When the smoke cleared, Bleeker had vanished.

Again Cannon swore, for everything hinged on Bleeker now. Catch him or kill him and this fight might end before anyone else got hurt.

A few yards away, Moore had seen Bleeker try to back-shoot him. He bawled, 'Get him, Tom! We'll cover you!'

As he, Tyson and Daniels set about doing just that, Cannon powered up and ran for the staircase, bullets chasing his heels all the way. He leapt over Valliere, kept going, taking the steps two at a time. As he reached the top, he was just in time to see Bleeker slam his office door. A second later he heard the sound of it being locked.

He went chasing along the corridor, got about halfway before Bleeker fired through the panels. He slammed his back against the wall, then kept going, aiming the shotgun at the lock even as he closed on it.

The shotgun blasted again and the lock and handle burst apart. He crashed into and through the door. Shattered wood flew everywhere as he near-fell into the room. Bleeker was behind his desk, his eyes round, scared. He brought his gun up and fired again.

The bullet missed, and Cannon slapped the shotgun to his shoulder and shouted, 'Drop it!'

Startled, Bleeker let the weapon fall to the floor and put his hands up. 'Wait!' he squealed. 'P . . . please, don't be hasty! You can still walk away from this with money in the bank!'

Cannon shook his head. 'Forget it, Lawrence. You're finished.'

Bleeker smiled bitterly. 'You're right.

Once those men downstairs get hold of me, they'll hang me from the tallest tree and then spit on my grave.'

'Can you blame them?'

Hatred flared back to life in his gaze. 'And who're you to sit in judgment of me?'

'I'm the man who came to find out what became of a man called Emmet Lawrence.'

'Well, you found out. Now you can go back to Frisco and tell Lorna the whole sorry story.'

'She deserves better than that,' said Cannon, adding quietly, 'And that's what she'll get.'

Bleeker frowned.

Cannon said, 'She might be all that you say she is and more besides, Lawrence. I don't know about that one way or the other. But for all her faults, she cared enough to pay good money to find out what became of you. When I get back to Frisco I'll make sure she knows.'

Bleeker licked his lips. 'That she

knows . . . ?' he prompted.

'That her husband died trying to do what he set out to do — make enough money to support her. That he was a good man, a man about whom other men spoke highly.'

'You'd do that for me?'

'I'm doing it for your wife.'

Bleeker looked down at the floor for a long moment. Finally, without looking up, he husked, 'Thank you.'

The sounds of gunfire were lessening now, becoming more sporadic. Someone, one of Bleeker's gunnies, called, 'All right! That's enough!'

A cheer rose up. Bleeker looked up, his eyes big now. 'Do me one more favour?' he said.

Already knowing the answer, Cannon said, 'What is it?'

Bleeker's voice broke. 'I don't want to hang.'

Cannon looked him straight in the eye and knew that he'd never said a truer word. 'There's a gun at your feet,' he said.

Footsteps started drumming on the stairs. Angry voices started yelling.

'Your time's up, Bleeker!'

'Get the bastard!'

'String him up!'

Bleeker bent and reached for the .45. Cannon's belly tightened.

Outside, Ezra Teal yelled, 'In here!'

Just as he and the rest of the miners started pouring into the room, Bleeker's lips moved soundlessly, and again he said, *Thank you.*

Then he shoved the gun up under his jaw and pulled the trigger.

Epilogue

It was a new day in Dawson. Down at the dock, Ezra Teal thrust out his right hand and said, 'Thanks again, Mr Cannon. If we'd have stormed the Monte Carlo like we planned to, a lot of folks would've died. Doin' it your way kept the damage to a minimum.'

'Yup,' said Joe Daniels, who was standing beside him. 'It's a shame that sonofabitch Bleeker cheated the hangrope, but I guess the important thing is that he's gone, an' Dawson'll be a better place without him.'

Cannon cut his gaze away to the tub boat that would be taking him on the first stage of the journey back to Dyea, and thence to San Francisco. He couldn't wait to get started, and if he never saw another flake of snow in his life, it would be too soon.

'So long, Ezra,' he said at length,

shaking with the big miner. 'You too, Joe. You've been a good friend.'

'Any time.'

He picked up his gear, wincing once at the protesting ache in his chest, then turned to Moore and Tyson. 'Better get going, fellers.'

The old man and the boy also gathered up their baggage, and then all three began to walk down to the jetty together.

'I still don't really know what to say, Mr Cannon,' said Tyson, glancing up at him. 'You had no need to give me a share of the money Bleeker's wife paid you to find him. I didn't do anythin' to earn it.'

'You stood by me through the whole thing, Jeff,' Cannon replied. 'You offered to side me when I went searching for Lawrence with that bushwhacking Tlingit. You saved my life when Valliere was fixing to kick me to death. And you did your share of the fighting at the Monte Carlo.'

'But $2,500!' said the lad. 'It's too much.'

'It's not nearly enough,' Cannon corrected him. 'But it'll give you, Susan and your baby that start you were after, and you can get back to them both all the sooner.' He threw a glance at Moore. 'And before you throw in your two cents' worth, Greybeard, you earned every penny you've got coming, as well.'

'Oh, I ain't gainsayin' that . . . '

'Glad to hear it. But I have to say, one thing still bothers me.'

'Oh?'

'Are you *sure* you've had your fill of gold-hunting at last?'

Moore glanced down at his broken arm. 'One thing this trip's taught me is that I'm not as young as I used to be. About time I put these old bones of mine out to rest.'

'You won't get much rest where you're goin', Greybeard,' laughed Tyson.

After the dust had settled over the Monte Carlo, Cannon had told both men that he'd be sharing his fee with them. Although they'd protested, his mind was made up. They'd earned it all right, and with his share of the money, there'd be no further need for Tyson to go seeking his fortune in the Yukon. That being the case, he'd decided to return to America with Cannon.

But he was reluctant to say goodbye to Moore. And when he'd told Moore that he wasn't getting any younger, and that he should start thinking about putting down roots with folks who'd care for him into his old age — him and Susan, for instance — the old man had been lost for words. Clearly moved, he'd gone off to be by himself for a while.

Over breakfast that morning, he'd finally accepted the invitation. 'So long as your Susan don't mind an old-timer clutterin' up the place.'

'Greybeard,' said Tyson, 'that's one thing you'll never have to worry about.'

They boarded the tub boat, stowed their gear below decks and then went topside again to take their last look at Dawson. The city was as busy as ever, a twenty-four-hour town where fortunes

— and lives — were made and lost by the minute.

For the citizens of Dawson, life went on as normal. And perhaps Lorna Lawrence would start to live again once she heard the lies Cannon would tell her when he got back to the Palace Hotel.

As for Cannon himself . . .

Well, as long as his beloved Amy remained trapped in the dark and silent world of the deafblind, Cannon would remain for hire.

We do hope that you have enjoyed reading this large print book.

Did you know that all of our titles are available for purchase?

We publish a wide range of high quality large print books including:
Romances, Mysteries, Classics
General Fiction
Non Fiction and Westerns

Special interest titles available in large print are:
The Little Oxford Dictionary
Music Book, Song Book
Hymn Book, Service Book

Also available from us courtesy of Oxford University Press:
Young Readers' Dictionary
(large print edition)
Young Readers' Thesaurus
(large print edition)

For further information or a free brochure, please contact us at:
Ulverscroft Large Print Books Ltd.,
The Green, Bradgate Road, Anstey,
Leicester, LE7 7FU, England.
Tel: (00 44) 0116 236 4325
Fax: (00 44) 0116 234 0205

DRIVE TO REDEMPTION

Mike Deane

Turning his back on drink and trouble making, Jim Boland returns to Ellsworth sober and ready to start a new life with Lucy, his girl. Unfortunately, the marshal who promised Jim a job is dead, and there's something sinister about his replacement. Unexpectedly, Marshal Jake Bradman makes him his deputy. However, will he turn a blind eye to Bradman's suspicious activities, and so remain in Ellsworth — or take his six-shooters, make his own investigations and seriously risk Lucy's life?